DEATH TRACKS THE SCENT

TESS BAYTREE

SPECULATIVE TURTLE PRESS

CHAPTER 1

The blue sky was sprinkled with puffy clouds, birds were chirping, and overall it was a beautiful day to be outside enjoying a brisk walk around the neighborhood. Or it would have been, if Penelope Standing hadn't been crouched behind a juniper bush, fending off an angry scrub jay. Also, the scrub jay wasn't chirping so much as screeching, and that would be a clear giveaway to anyone who knew birds. She needed to find another place to hide.

Mailbag banging against her hip, Penelope sprinted to the next house, reflecting that she didn't have as much speed in her fifties as she'd had in younger years, but she certainly was a lot more motivated. She shoved the handful of mail — lots of pink envelopes; Harold Stone wasn't paying his bills, and wasn't that interesting? — into the slot on the door and dove behind the overgrown tea tree shrub next to the house. It was a good hiding place to get the next batch of mail ready.

Avoiding people while walking dogs was easier. She could either take a different path, or just literally run away and claim that she hadn't heard anyone calling. Delivering mail caused more difficulties, especially when she was covering the same route for an entire week. The mail truck, an ancient model used only by fill-in carriers, was a dead giveaway that she was in the neighborhood.

"Mayor Standing! Yoo hoo!" Lorna Harvey was on the opposite side of the street, facing the wrong direction, so Penelope stayed where she was.

Lorna Harvey was one of those people who didn't take no for an answer. She didn't take anything for an answer. She expected her targets to do whatever she asked, immediately. In that, she wasn't all that different from a lot of people in town. Penelope had lived there almost thirty years, had divorced there, raised a child there, and remarried there, and she knew the inhabitants as well as anyone.

The difference with Lorna was that she took her complaints to a whole new level *and* she had a heart condition that occasionally made her pass out. The local plumber would no longer go to her house after her loud and long-winded reaction to the emergency charge. The police officer knocking on her door to tell her she couldn't fly her drone over her neighbor's house to record their parties had spent the next hour listening to her rants because he saw a purple tinge to her lips and was worried she was dying.

Penelope had been pulled into her orbit when Lorna had shown up at a city council session Penelope had presided over. Lorna had demanded to be allowed to erect a seven foot wall around her front lawn. The barrier would have blocked access to the water shutoff, violated a handful of codes, and cut off light to her neighbor's vegetable garden. Lorna got so worked up while speaking to the captive audience that she turned blue and fainted. While the EMTs were checking on Lorna, Penelope had hurried through the rest of the docket, and all the elected officials had fled without their usual after-meeting arguments.

That had been three months ago. Even though Penelope

was no longer mayor — big developer money had caused a course correction at the next regular election — Lorna was still trying to corner her to plead her case. And for someone with such an extensive medical history, Lorna was *fast*.

The next house was only getting two circulars and a welcome notice from the new insurance broker downtown. It seemed a shame to get stuck dealing with Lorna for the sake of mail that was probably immediately going into the recycle bin, but that wasn't a call Penelope could make. She parted a branch to check on Lorna's progress. Lorna was still across the street, and still looking around.

Harold really was letting his front yard go. The Swiss chard had overflowed its bed, the basil was nearly dead, and unless she was mistaken, there was Bermuda grass strangling the sage. Even the bush she was hiding behind was in need of trimming. That was unusual.

Harold Stone's religion was natural food, and his shop, Homespun Harold's All-Natural Emporium, was the pulpit from which he preached. According to him, natural products were the cure for everything, and anything "unnatural" caused everything from cancer to alcoholism. The area in front of his house had always been a beautiful showcase of everything a man could need to stay healthy. Penelope noticed that he didn't have a problem using an automated watering system in his herb garden. Maybe some plastics were more organic than others.

A loud bark right behind her shoulder made Penelope jump. She glanced back and saw Harold's black Labrador retriever, Crunch, his face inches from hers. Crunch had the clear eyes and sharp white teeth of a young dog. Penelope blew out a breath. She knew Crunch from the dog park. Even if he hadn't been on the other side of the glass, he'd never harm her. He might accidentally run into her while playing, but that was expected at the park, and the one time he'd managed to knock her off her feet, he'd licked her face in apology. Penelope really liked Crunch, even if his owner wasn't her favorite person. Right now, the Lab's forehead was wrinkled in worry.

"I'm sorry, buddy," she whispered. "I'll move away from the window as soon as Lorna goes away. You're a good dog."

Crunch let his front feet drop from the window sill and raced away and then back, barking all the while.

Penelope winced. She couldn't blame Crunch for barking at an intruder, but the last thing she needed was to have Harold come outside to find out why she was hiding in the bushes staring through his window. Harold was a notorious pain to deal with under normal circumstances; Penelope couldn't imagine how he would react in this case. She had dog treats with her — Penelope *always* had dog treats with her — but there was no way to get them to Crunch to stop his barking.

Crunch's barks changed to an urgent whine, and Penelope looked back at him, hoping that speaking to him again would make him calm down. But Crunch wasn't at the window. Instead, he was nosing something on the floor, a large grey dog toy, with silver tufts that looked like hair…

Penelope swallowed, no longer worried about Lorna finding her there. That wasn't a dog toy making Crunch whine. That was Hippie Harold, lying on the floor of his living room.

And he looked very, very dead.

CHAPTER 2

The call to emergency services was quick. The dispatcher didn't identify herself, but her voice was half-familiar, and Penelope was fairly certain she knew her. She gave her name, and the address, and said she could see someone lying on the floor who didn't appear to be breathing.

"The fire department is on the way. Are there signs of violence?" The dispatcher paused as if trying to figure out how to word the next part. "It sounds like you're whispering. Are you in a safe place?"

Penelope cleared her throat and spoke a little louder. "No. I mean yes, I'm safe, I think. I don't see any signs of violence. But I'm hiding in the bushes trying to avoid Lorna Harvey."

There was a slightly longer pause and all the background chatter disappeared. Penelope suspected the dispatcher had gone on mute because she was laughing, but when she spoke again her voice was professional. "You should be able to hear the sirens soon. Can you stay there and show them what you saw?" When Penelope assented, the line went dead.

The dispatcher had definitely recognized her, and though

Penelope could hear the sirens, they were at least a mile away, which meant she still had a chance to make her second call before Jake heard about this through other means. She tapped his number.

Her husband picked up on the second ring. "I'm in a meeting. Is this an emergency?"

"No. I just wanted to let you know that I'm fine and I didn't kill him."

"Why are you whispering?" Then Jake paused. "Who didn't you kill? Do you need a lawyer?"

One of the many things she loved about Jake was his ability to focus on the important things. "Hippie Harold. And I don't think so." The sirens were getting louder. "I'll tell you about it tonight. Enjoy your meeting."

She hung up. That had gone well. Jake had been a bit depressed about retiring, though he'd tried to hide it. Now she'd given him something different to think about during his last day on the job. Selfless tasks like that were what made marriage work.

Penelope waited where she was until the front of the firetruck blocked her view of Lorna, and then stepped out and waved from the sidewalk. Two of the men jogged up the path. One she recognized as the little brother of one of her son's friends from high school, though she couldn't remember his name. It was something like Braden. Or Aiden? So many of their names had rhymed that she'd had a hard time keeping them straight. Somehow he'd gotten old enough that he probably had children of his own to go with his receding hairline.

"Hi, Ms. Standing. You said you could see someone inside? Can you show us?"

Penelope beckoned them over to the window. "You might have to move a couple of branches." The other fireman, the one who wasn't something that rhymed with Aiden — maybe

Jayden? — looked a little puzzled, but his partner didn't hesitate. He stepped up to the window, pushed a handful of greenery out of the way, then jumped back as Crunch's snarling face filled the pane.

"Ah, yeah." He looked at the other man. "Elderly male on the floor."

Penelope stared at him. Elderly? Harold was younger than she was.

The firefighter didn't notice her look. "Let's see if we can find an open door. And we'll have to figure out a way to deal with the dog."

From the lack of urgency in his voice, Penelope assumed he agreed with her about it being too late for Harold. She couldn't do anything about that, but she could help with the other part of the problem. "If you can open the door, I can probably grab Crunch for you. He knows me from the dog park." The Lab was also less likely to feel threatened by a woman than a man, but she didn't say that part out loud.

None of the doors were unlocked, so they opened the front door with a Halligan bar. The moment the frame cracked and the door popped open, a burglar alarm started a repetitive beep, notifying them that they needed to enter a code to disarm it. At the same time Crunch ran forward to the gap, barking and growling.

Penelope elbowed her way forward and pulled out her bag of treats. "Hey there, Crunch. Remember me?" She tossed a treat toward him and was relieved when he grabbed it off the floor. Holding another one in her hand, she moved a closed fist upward in the same sign she'd seen Harold use. "Sit." The dog sat, and she tossed him another treat, which he caught out of the air, and then stood up again. Penelope could see a leash on the side table next to the door. She held it up. "Go for a walk? Hm?"

Crunch moved forward, tail wagging, though he was still

looking at the firemen behind her. She clipped his leash on and led him outside, passing him three more treats in the time it took her to get him to the driveway where there was a little more room. He stopped to lift his leg on a sage plant. From the looks of things, he'd been inside for a long time. "Such a good boy." She scratched behind his ears and he leaned into her.

From the sidewalk closer to the door she heard one of the firemen ask that the coroner be notified. That answered that question then. Penelope supposed she should be sad about a life that had been lost, but mostly she just felt relief that she wouldn't have to deal with another lecture on the evils of commercial dog food when she just wanted to relax at the dog park.

"Mayor Standing!"

Penelope closed her eyes. In the excitement of learning how they opened a locked door, and then grabbing Crunch, she'd forgotten about Lorna Harvey. "Not anymore." She opened her eyes just in time to see Lorna trip on the curb next to the back of the firetruck, and one of the firemen — Kayden, that was it — reach forward and grab her before she fell.

"Careful, Mrs. Harvey. You might have fallen and hit your head. The coroner doesn't give us any two for one specials, you know."

Penelope ducked her head to hide a laugh and concentrated on scratching Crunch's rear end. A cough closer to the door told her that the other firefighters had heard Kayden's remark.

Kayden's voice stayed gentle, though, and she remembered how kind he had been even as a boy following the older kids around. "Why don't you have a seat on the bumper here, Mrs. Harvey, just until you're sure you have your balance back."

Penelope expected Lorna to take the opportunity to recite her complaints, but no. Apparently Kayden had just the right touch, and the two of them sat down together.

That solved one of Penelope's problems, but now she had a different one. She gave Crunch another treat. Presumably there would be a relative or friend who would provide a new home for Crunch. That assumed Harold *had* any friends, which she found hard to believe, although maybe he had some redeeming qualities since he had a nice dog. In any case, Penelope needed to deliver the mail, and Crunch could probably use some exercise. Also, that would get her farther away in case Lorna suddenly came to her senses.

Penelope waved to catch Kayden's attention, and when he looked up, she made a motion to indicate circling the block and mouthed "five minutes." He nodded in understanding, and she headed to the next house, Crunch in tow. She didn't doubt the police would want to get a statement, but they weren't there yet. Besides, they all knew where she lived.

The Hernandezes weren't getting any mail for their daughter, Anna, anymore, which meant she had moved out and it was being forwarded somewhere. Penelope hoped she'd gone back to college and not to her boyfriend in the Navy, but nineteen was the age to make big mistakes and hopefully learn something from them. Better that than to have a sudden wild streak in her mid-thirties when there were children involved.

The tenants at the cottage behind one-nineteen — officially one-nineteen and a half — were fond of online shopping. She'd already dropped a stack of boxes off near their door, but they also received colorful catalogs full of novelty items that cost less than a cup of coffee for a bag of fifty. Someday Penelope would figure out what they did with all of it, but that was a mystery for later.

Crunch trotted along by her side, occasionally stopping

to mark a tree or a section of grass.

They were rounding the corner when a police car stopped at the curb. Penelope waited for the officer to get out. He was a tall, thin man, and Penelope knew they'd been introduced at some point, but she couldn't remember his name.

She could tell exactly the point when he recognized her, though. His shoulders drooped. "Oh. Hi, Mrs. Wheeler."

With an effort, Penelope kept from gritting her teeth. "It's Ms. Standing. After half a century, I'm pretty used to my own name." It irked her that nobody ever assumed Jake would have changed *his* name even though both of them had gotten married.

The officer stared at her, and she realized she'd derailed his train of thought. Good.

"Did you need me for something?" She shortened Crunch's leash so he couldn't pee on the nearest tire.

"No. Well… We had a call about someone sneaking around in the bushes and looking in windows, and I heard there was a dead body nearby, and…" He trailed to a stop, clearly having second thoughts about explaining himself, even if she was the assistant chief's wife.

"Nope." Penelope held up the envelopes in her hand. "Just me delivering the mail." He looked new enough that he might not know Lorna Harvey yet, and she didn't feel like trying to explain. She held back on congratulating his foresight in thinking there might be a connection. He would see it as patronizing instead of the encouragement of what her son called "mom mode."

"Sorry to have bothered you. Have a nice day." He was back in the car before she could say anything, so she just smiled and waved with the hand holding the envelopes, and let Crunch have the slack he needed to move forward and pee on the tire.

CHAPTER 3

*B*y the time Penelope had done the cloverleaf pattern that she normally travelled to deliver in the area and had headed back to Harold's house, three police cars were parked at the curb, and the firetruck was completing a U-turn at the intersection. The driver tapped the horn and waved, and Penelope was briefly filled with an intense longing to once, just once, ride around town in one of the rear-facing seats of the fire engine. She sighed and waved back. When her son had been a toddler, he had been the perfect reason to tour places, and do things like slide down the fire pole, or see how the conductor drove a train. Now she didn't have a good excuse.

Lieutenant Brian Keegan, one of Jake's closest friends, was leaning on a car, hands shoved in his pockets, a point of calm in the busy scene. Penelope knew Brian was supposed to be training and evaluating his replacement, but she hadn't thought he could hold himself back from taking over.

He stood up when he saw her, and raised an eyebrow at the dog. "Didn't you end up with the dog the last time you found a body too?"

"You make it sound like I do that sort of thing all the time." She stopped and fed Crunch another treat. If she couldn't pass him off to someone soon, she'd have to go back to the mail truck to replenish her supply. "I offered to grab Crunch when the firemen broke in since I know him from the dog park."

"Does Jake know you two have a new dog?"

Penelope held up a finger. "First of all, Brutus is all Jake's fault, not mine." She stopped when she saw his lips twitch. "And second, I figure Harold must have some family or friends… well, family anyhow," she amended with a grimace, "that will take him."

Brian's eyes sharpened. "You knew the deceased?"

"It sounds bad when you say it like that. Everybody knew Harold." When Brian's expression didn't change, she cocked her head to the side. "Harold Stone?" Still no response. "Hippie Harold?"

His face cleared. "The guy from the natural shop downtown?"

"See! He's probably yelled at you at least once, too. It's not just me." Harold might not have been the undisputed town crank, but that was only because there were so many of them in the running. She fed Crunch another treat.

"Huh. I told them to treat it as a suspicious death just as a training exercise while we're waiting for the coroner, but maybe we should keep it that way." Brian pulled his notebook from his jacket pocket. "Do you know if he had any family?"

"Two kids, I think. I guess they'd be in their mid-twenties…" She paused. "Maybe late twenties." Possibly older than that, but she remembered seeing them as toddlers at some school play so it seemed like they shouldn't even be adults yet. "His ex-wife still lives in town, but I think she remarried and I don't know what her new name is."

Brian smothered a grin and Penelope cleared her throat. He was well-aware of her feelings on the societal expectations for women to change their names. She ignored him and continued. "And I've seen his daughter in the shop. I'm not sure if his son is still in the area." His son had been in rehab at least once before he'd dropped out of high school. Harold had seen the problem, which couldn't be solved with whole grains or essential oils, as deliberate rebellion. Penelope hadn't seen, or at least hadn't recognized, Harold's son in years.

Brian looked past her at something going on near the front door of the house, then took a deep breath and let it out before focussing on her again. "You were delivering mail when you saw him?"

Penelope nodded. "Marcia's in Barbados for two weeks, and nobody wants to fill in on the downtown routes, so I've been here five days in a row." Normally she only filled in a few days a month, and usually ended up on a different route each time. This had been an interesting change.

"And you just happened to see him when you passed by?"

"It's not like I was looking through the window hoping to see a body."

Brian's eyes flicked to the doorway and back. "Pen." He raised his eyebrows. "There are branches covering half the window and with the glare and the angle, you can't see his body unless you're a couple inches from the glass."

"You should be grateful. Imagine how it would be if nobody noticed for another day or two." When Brian merely continued to stare at her, she gave in. "Fine. I was hiding in the bushes because Lorna Harvey was stalking me. She's mad at me because I wouldn't let her build a drawbridge and a moat, or whatever, around her house. I'm avoiding her. She almost died at that council meeting, and with my luck she'll drop dead right in front of me and there won't be any witnesses." She stopped when she realized Brian was laughing. "You already knew about Lorna, didn't you?"

He made an effort to look serious. "The dispatchers talk. A lot. Plus we got a call about a suspicious person hiding in the bushes, and the description is a pretty close match." He looked at her bright pink running shoes. "If you ever decide to switch to a life of crime, ditch the shoes."

A white SUV pulled into the driveway, and a thin woman with long brown hair got out. She turned her head to look at the police cars. "What's going on?"

Penelope avoided her gaze. "That's his daughter, Skye," she murmured. Brian had already walked away from her, heading to break the news to Harold's daughter, when Penelope realized she still had the dog. She couldn't just tie Crunch up and leave, and now was probably not the appropriate time to hand him off to Skye. She resigned herself to another wait.

Skye gave a loud cry. "No! He was fine yesterday!" She wobbled on her feet, though Penelope noticed she managed a graceful collapse into the seat of her SUV, which required a little hop. Penelope wondered if she was being unkind. Harold had been Skye's father, and even if he'd been a pain in the rear to society at large, there were some bonds that defied logic. Besides, people handled grief differently, and a performative aspect might just mean the reality hadn't set in and she knew she was supposed to react in some way.

The county coroner's van pulled over, blocking in the SUV.

For all the extra people who were now at Harold's house, Penelope still didn't see anyone she could hand Crunch off to. She sighed and waved to get Brian's attention, then repeated her gesture of circling the block. He nodded, and she set off with Crunch again.

This time she had to walk back to the elderly mail truck

first, both to get the next set of mail to deliver, and to refill her treat bag. Luckily, Crunch was young and healthy. A few extra miles of walking would do him good, especially on a stressful day like this.

* * *

ONE MORE CLOVERLEAF DONE, PENELOPE AND CRUNCH headed back to the house. The coroner's van was gone, one of the police cars had disappeared, and another car, a blue BMW sedan with an incongruous bumper sticker declaring "Homespun Harold's Natural Products: Live Clean, Love Life", had parked in the neighborhood of the curb. Skye and Amelia, her mother, stood by the SUV, watching as a gurney went by, the remains enclosed in a black body bag.

Skye sobbed loudly as the gurney went past, and her mother reached out to pat her shoulder, but almost as if she was an actor who knew the stage directions yet couldn't quite nail down the motivation. Penelope had always found family dynamics fascinating.

She checked the time. If she didn't get moving on the rest of her route, she'd have to stop in the middle and drive the mail truck over to give a cat insulin, which was definitely against the rules. Not that she'd ever been big on following rules, but she wasn't getting anything done standing around here, and there was always the danger that Lorna Harvey might come back. Brian excused himself from the two women and went into the house, giving Penelope her chance. She walked over to them.

"Amelia, Skye, I'm so sorry for your loss." That part was easy, because that was the acceptable thing to say even if the dead man had once spent five minutes following her around the park ranting about GMOs because she'd mentioned using popcorn as a treat in a conversation he hadn't even been involved in. She held up the end of Crunch's leash. "I was holding on to Crunch so the firemen could check on Harold, but I really need to get back to work now. Can I leave him with you?"

Amelia reached out to take the leash when her daughter didn't move. "Harold had a dog?" That, more than anything else, seemed to throw her off. "But I was the one who always wanted a dog when we were married. He said they were too much extra chaos." She looked at the house in confusion.

Skye still hadn't looked at the dog. If anything, she looked annoyed that Penelope had interrupted their conversation. Penelope did the internal equivalent of a shrug. Some people just weren't animal people. She'd try not to hold that against Skye, though she knew that effort would fail.

Penelope addressed her words to Amelia. "This is Crunch. He's a very good boy." She handed over her plastic bag of treats and one of her dog walking business cards. "If you have questions about him, or need a referral to a veterinarian, my number's on there. I only really know Crunch from the dog park, but that's probably better than nothing."

Amelia looked at her card. "Penelope. I thought I recognized you. Sorry." When Penelope waved the apology away, she smiled. "How is your son doing?"

"He's doing well. He writes games now." Penelope stopped herself. This probably wasn't the time to catch up with Amelia. "Call me if you need anything." She leaned down to scratch Crunch's ears again. "You behave yourself, young man."

Straightening, she walked away, lifted a hand to wave to Brian, and then headed off to cover the rest of her route. She had handed off the dog and that concluded her part. The professionals could handle the rest.

She crossed her fingers behind her back even as she thought it.

CHAPTER 4

The best part about this particular mail carrier route was that she could plan it out so she finished at Esther's house. She needed to go there anyhow to scoop litter boxes and do any cat care that required agility or heavy lifting, but it was nice to finish up all the walking with a few moments to sit and hear the latest gossip, with fresh lemonade or hot tea, depending on the weather. After that she would have just enough time to drop off the mail truck and get over to her next client's house without giving the grumpy old cat any real reason to complain about his food not being available at his preferred time.

A young man was leaving Esther's house as Penelope walked up the ramp, and she smiled at him. He seemed vaguely familiar in that way that many young people did. He looked a bit like a more youthful version of that one actor on the show about the hikers, but that was the only clue her brain decided to give her, and it wasn't helpful. She'd probably watched him in any number of terrible school plays and musical performances while waiting for a chance to see her son. Esther had taught kindergarten for nearly forty years, and she still kept in touch with a lot of the families even though she'd been retired for over two decades.

Penelope knocked, then opened the door after Esther called for her to come in. She paused on the way to the kitchen to pick up Frito, the white Persian cat who loved to sit on shoulders. Frito hadn't finished sniffing her shirt when she got to the kitchen where Esther was wheeling herself back to the kitchen table with a pitcher of lemonade.

"I hear you had quite the morning," Esther said as she began pouring. "First Lorna Harvey, and then poor Harold."

That Esther already knew about Harold wasn't a surprise; the town's gossip mill was always active, and *real* news sent it into overdrive. Because she had difficulty moving around, Esther had become a hub for information. She had probably had at least seven visits, in-person or via phone, in the two hours since Penelope had first called 911.

"Poor Harold?" Penelope had known Esther long enough to hear from her tone that Harold hadn't been her favorite person. That wasn't a surprise. Harold hadn't been *anybody's* favorite person. Esther was kind, but she wasn't stupid. "Which thing did he yell at you about?"

Esther smiled. "Oh, no. We never had words like that." She sighed. "I taught both his children. Some people should never be parents."

Penelope thought about her ex-husband. "If everyone had to pass a test before having children, the human race might die out." She shook her head. "Let me guess. Natural food will cure dyslexia?"

"No, I had both his children before he stopped drinking and became all-natural. And they were both ahead, at least academically. But Edward — he was still called Bear then — had such anxieties. He was forever being set up to take the blame for things the other children did, and he always accepted it." She stopped to sip her lemonade. "That sort of thing isn't good for anybody involved. It can be hard to determine at that age what is just normal behavior that they will grow out of, and what needs intervention. But I thought Bear ought to see an individual counselor, or at the very least, have a few family sessions."

"I'm guessing that didn't go over well." Then something Esther had said struck Penelope. "Harold used to drink?" And drink enough that it had been a problem, or Esther wouldn't have mentioned it.

"Harold was famous for closing down the bars. By the time he quit, he'd lost his job and his license, and they would have lost the house if Amelia hadn't been working so much. Then there was a fire — he passed out with a lit cigarette — and Amelia threatened to leave him if he didn't stop." She grinned wryly. "Some men find God, others Alcoholics Anonymous, and Harold found bean sprouts and recycling."

Penelope had no problem imagining Harold as a sidewalk preacher. He'd had the same fervor. She lifted Frito and set her carefully on the floor. "I should get moving." As she headed toward the litter boxes in the guest room, she continued their conversation. "I saw his daughter at the house. How is his son doing these days?"

"Very well. He found therapy and AA. He's been sober for five years and just got engaged to a very nice girl. You passed him on your way in the door."

Penelope paused in her scooping so she could turn to look over her shoulder at Esther. "That was Bear?" A less Bear-like person she'd never encountered.

Esther nodded at her unspoken words. "He goes by his middle name, Edward, now. A much better fit, I think."

Penelope had almost finished when the name rearranged

itself in her head. "I guess it could be worse. They could have named him Edward Bear and he'd have been stuck with Teddy Bear all his life."

"And it *still* wouldn't have been the worst name I saw while I was teaching. Now tell me how that young man of yours is doing. Has he decided what he's going to do next?"

Penelope reminded herself to tell Jake he retained his young man status. "He's still thinking about it. Or rather, he seems to think that he's really retiring and he'll just relax every day." Her laugh was echoed in Esther's snort behind her. "I give him three weeks before he's applying to be a greeter at the hardware store, if that's the only thing available."

"If it comes down to that, let me know. I have a list of volunteer jobs that need someone who can get things done. But hopefully he'll find his own path." Esther sighed. "So many men tie up their entire sense of self and community with their career and then have no idea who they are after they stop working.

A random tidbit bubbled up in Penelope's thoughts. "Did you know, the Italians have a word to describe the old men who stand around outside a construction site and comment on how the work is going?" The exact word escaped her, but that wasn't too surprising. Some days her English vocabulary took a vacation, and that was her *first* language. "Although I guess that means they have friends to gather with. Italian men aren't the ones who have to play golf because they need an excuse to invite a friend on a walk."

Esther laughed again, then sobered. "Don't get me wrong — some women are like that with raising their children. But they don't lose all their friends when their children leave home."

Penelope stood and stretched her back. "I'm fairly confident of my ability to be annoying enough that he'll find something to do just to get out of the house. But if not, we'll go over that list. There must be something on there that will keep him from spending his days sitting on the couch drinking beer."

CHAPTER 5

*M*ired in the final stretch of packing up his office, Jake looked like he was ready for a few weeks of sitting on a couch and drinking beer. Or possibly something stronger. Penelope leaned against the doorframe and watched as her husband scribbled a signature, then tried to decide which of the overflowing piles on his desk to place the folder on. The walls looked strangely bare without the awards, pictures, and certificates that normally hung there. Brutus bounded forward to put his paws on Jake's shoulders, his bulk nearly overbalancing the chair. Penelope put a hand out to keep the nearest stack of folders from sliding to the ground.

Jake let the chair lean backward while he scratched the mastiff's jowls. "Who's my best boy?" He had to move his face to the side to avoid the worst of the licking that followed. He pitched his voice so Penelope could hear him. "Brian said you didn't seem too shaken up after finding the body." He moved Brutus's head out of the way so he could see her. "You okay?"

"I'm fine." Penelope thought about it. She'd certainly been far more disturbed when she'd found Jezza's body, but that time she'd been in the same room and it clearly hadn't been a natural death. "The first one was more of a shock."

"It might be better not to make a habit of it." Jake shoved Brutus to the side so he could sit up.

"I'd rather not. If I'm going to develop new habits, I'd rather have them be fun things. Speaking of which, do you think they would let me ride on the firetruck in one of the rear-facing seats if I asked?" At Jake's raised eyebrow, she shrugged. "It just looks like it might be fun. Never mind. I was just walking your dog on the long route because it looked like he made it through the day without getting into anything he shouldn't. Since we were here anyhow, I thought I'd stop in and see if you needed any help."

Jake stood, picked up one stack of files, and then paused. "What did he do on the walk that turned him from a *good* dog into *my* dog?"

"He seems to have eaten a box of crayons at some point in the past day or so. Did you have a stash somewhere?"

Jake went past her and shoved the folders into an organizer hanging from the side of the absent admin's desk. "Not that I remember."

"I don't remember any either, but your dog is pooping rainbows now. I'm sure we'll figure it out at some point."

Jake paused in moving folders around to cradle Brutus's head. "Who's my good little unicorn?" Then he glanced up at her. "Crayons aren't bad for him, right?"

Penelope waved that worry away. "Kids eat them all the time. I'm a little more worried about what else he might have gotten into at the same time, but I guess if he mugged a small child it shouldn't be too bad." She followed Jake's sight line to Brian who had walked up behind her. "Hello again."

"Hi, Pen." He edged past her to go inside Jake's office. "I know you're just about out of here, but Chief Purcell is out until tomorrow and his voice mailbox is full and he has that thing about verbal communication so I'm just going to tell you so I can say I told someone."

There was an air of grim determination to act like professionals filling the office, so Penelope kept her mouth shut. Even though she'd been the mayor at the time Chief Purcell had been hired, as the wife of the acting police chief, Penelope had recused herself from the decision making process. The council's choice hadn't been in her top three — she'd been aiming for a more progressive candidate. Now they all had to live with the consequences.

At Jake's nod, Brian continued. "The post is scheduled for first thing in the morning. Initial thoughts at the scene were that he had some medical event and was too drunk to call for help, but the coroner got all excited about all the home canned food. I guess nobody dies from botulism anymore and it's a big deal if it happens."

"But —" Penelope brought herself up short. They hadn't asked for her opinion and she wasn't even supposed to be here.

Brian turned to look at her. "Out with it."

"Harold stopped drinking decades ago."

"His whole house reeked of alcohol."

Penelope suddenly remembered the untended herb garden. Maybe he had fallen off the wagon. "But even if he had started drinking again, there's just no way he would have gotten botulism from something he canned. He taught classes. He knew what he was doing."

Brian cocked his head. "You know, you're the first person to say something nice about him all day."

Penelope let out a long breath. "And it didn't even kill me."

"Okay, but my understanding is that even with perfect technique you can still get botulism."

"Yes." Penelope dropped Brutus's leash, since there

wasn't anywhere for him to go and she needed her hands to mime the technique. "When you can something, you sterilize the jars and fill them with whatever you're canning. And then you add the lid and the ring." She put the lid and ring on an invisible Ball jar. "Then you boil it or put it in a pressure cooker, which should kill off any bacteria inside."

"Pen, my grandmother used to can venison stew, and she was meticulous, but I still remember finding a moldy jar in her cupboard after she died."

"Yes, but she never would have eaten it. The important part is that after the jars cool down, you take the rings off so if gas builds up in the jar the lid pops off and it's obvious that it's spoiled. You only run into problems if someone leaves the ring holding the top on, or they stack the jars so there's external pressure holding the top in place." She dropped her hands. "I'll bet you a hundred dollars you didn't find anything like that at Harold's house."

Brian frowned thoughtfully. "No. He had special shelving in the pantry so each jar had half an inch of space above it. And no rings."

Harold had shown a picture of his pantry during the canning class Penelope had taken, so she could easily picture it. "I'd believe space aliens killed him before I'd believe he died from botulism. Heck, I'd believe he *was* a space alien before I'd believe he died from botulism." She reached down to pick up Brutus's leash. "The autopsy will probably show he had a heart attack caused by the stress of yelling at everyone for everything."

Brian sighed. "I guess I'll find out tomorrow morning." He looked over at Jake again. "Any thoughts?"

"No, just keep me updated… No. Assuming it comes back as natural causes, don't forget to release the scene." Jake looked down at his desk and then brightened. He scooped up the largest stack of folders and pressed them on Brian. "I'll let you take these."

"You know I'm only here for another week, right?"

"They just need a final check and a signature." He added another folder onto the stack. "Plus the non-urgent citizen complaints." He looked at the desk again, and Brian edged toward the door.

Penelope moved out of the way to let Brian get away before he had any more work dumped on him. "Are you still planning on coming home for dinner, or should I assume it's just me and the unicorn?"

"Just give me a couple of minutes..." Jake frowned at his desk and sighed. "It's probably going to be just you and the unicorn."

There were definitely parts of his job that Penelope wasn't going to miss. "Don't stay too late. They know where to find you if they have questions later." She tugged on Brutus's leash. "Come on, you. Let's go see if you fart out some gold on the way home."

CHAPTER 6

*E*arly in the morning, the rectory kitchen of the Episcopal church smelled of coffee, sugar, and elderly Dalmatian, a mixture that Penelope would have bottled and worn as her signature scent, if she'd been the type to have a signature scent. Or worn perfume at all.

Rays of light skipped around the dust on the windows, picking out the path worn into the floor between the table and the refrigerator. The linoleum closer to the walls, where Penelope was sitting, was in better shape, though some child had modified the gamboling lambs of the pattern years ago to add devil's horns and tails with a red permanent marker, so the whole floor was unusual, to say the least. Penelope had spent a lot of time looking at the floor over the years as she kept Spot company while Reverent CJ Miller held services in the building next door.

"This retirement thing is great." Jake sat next to her on the floor, with Spot's head on one leg, a slightly stale donut in one hand, and a mug of coffee in the other. "I should have done this years ago."

The rest of the Dalmatian's body was flopped over Penelope's lap. She paused on the brink of pointing out that it was still the morning before his first missed shift, and decided to keep that thought to herself. "If you had retired years ago, how would you have kept me in the style to which I've become accustomed?" She broke off a piece of his donut and popped it in her mouth.

He leaned over to kiss her temple. "I'm pretty certain I could dust off my guitar and play for tips downtown and still keep you happy."

"Running shoes are expensive. Besides, I could do that too."

"Yes, but people would be paying *me* to keep playing, not to make me stop."

Penelope waved that fact away. "Po-tay-to po-tah-to." She scratched Spot's chest, and the dog's tail thumping against the floor was the only sound for a bit apart from Jake's phone, which had been buzzing with incoming messages all morning. "Are you sure you don't need me to do anything for the party?" She wasn't scheduled to deliver mail, and while she had a full day of pet sitting and dog walking duties planned, she could free up time if she needed to.

"It's all in hand. I'll do a final pass of the yard to pick up any more unicorn poop this afternoon, but the caterers are taking care of everything else. And I'll take the unicorn himself out for a run after lunch so he's too tired to be a pest at the party."

Penelope looked at him. He was serious. "You really think you can wear out our dog to the point where he's going to sleep through an event with dozens of people who might be tricked into feeding him?"

Jake raised an eyebrow. "Are you really insulting my manhood like that?"

"Never! I happen to love your manhood. It's your knees I'm worried about. Brutus is a *terrible* jogging partner. He runs by your side just long enough to lull you into believing he'll stay there, and then he barges through you to get to something on the other side." She'd been working on it, but Brutus was the mastiff embodiment of the spirit being willing but the flesh being weak. He tried to be good, but his brain was easily short-circuited by his nose.

"We'll be fine. I outweigh him."

"He has a lower center of gravity. Just be careful. If you fall down and hit your head, Purcell will find some way to pin it on me, and then who will look after Brutus? He already has abandonment issues."

"I'm pretty sure the only abandonment issue Brutus has is that chicken wing he found in the bushes a month ago at Oak and Greenway. I made him drop it and he's still checking for it. Besides, if you and Purcell ever went head to head, my money's on you." His phone buzzed again, and he put his coffee down to pull up the messages. "Stone's lawyer must have loved him."

It took Penelope a moment to realize he was talking about Harold. "Lawsuits?"

"And restraining orders, both requested by him and against him. I'm a little surprised your name isn't in the mix."

"I mostly just avoided him." Penelope tried to muster some offense at being called out like that but gave it up. She did have a contentious history with quite a few of the town's odder citizens. "But why are they texting you about it? You're retired."

"Brian's just sending me the funnier highlights. The janitor at city hall had a restraining order against him last year. Stone wasn't allowed to come within fifty feet of the building after hours. I can understand personality conflicts, but this seems to have been related to the man's job. Who picks a fight with the janitor?"

"That's easy." Penelope stole the last of his donut with the reasoning that if he wanted more he was free to get up and get one, whereas she was weighed down by the dog in her lap. "Harold really only had two windmills he liked to tilt at."

"Mm, literary references. Sexy body *and* mind."

"Cliff's Notes helped me convince my son I was smarter than him when he was a teenager." She paused to chew. "Harold was anti-chemical…" She held up a hand when Jake opened his mouth. "I know, I know. Everything is a chemical. But he was one of those people who thought natural was synonymous with healthy, and if the name of an ingredient was hard to pronounce, it must cause cancer, or some syndrome that doctors all knew the cause of but wouldn't tell their patients about because of some conspiracy involving pharmaceutical companies." She paused again to take a sip of coffee. "He probably wanted city hall to use vinegar and lemons to clean everything. But I doubt the janitor controls any of that, so that's not what their scuffle was about."

"And windmill number two?"

"Recycling. He would scream at total strangers for putting their glass bottles in the trash downtown. They banned him from the minimarket because he would have meltdowns in the aisle when some product was using plastic that was classified as number five, which couldn't be recycled. He's the reason the town had a recycling program long before it was common. It wasn't because he led the effort, though. It was because everyone just wanted him to quit bugging them."

"Some people are jewels, others are meant to be the irritating grit that causes a pearl to form."

"Maybe you can write greeting cards in your next career." She took another sip of coffee. "Or epitaphs. There must be money in that somehow."

"So his problem with the janitor…" Jake was better at remembering the point of the conversation than she was.

"Definitely recycling. My guess is that he found out that

when the janitor made his rounds to empty all the individual waste baskets and recycling bins in the building, everything was getting dumped into the same big trash can. It's the dirty little secret of a lot of corporate and government buildings."

Jake turned to look at her, leaning back so he could focus on her face. "What?"

"Someone important, or just really irritating, demands a recycling program, so they buy special waste baskets, print a bunch of flyers, pat themselves on the back, and brag about their recycling program. Meanwhile, nobody's put any thought into how the people who have to clean the entire building in an hour every night are going to deal with it all. It's an implementation problem, but I can guarantee you that Harold would have blamed the janitor."

Penelope lapsed into silence again, listening to Spot's tail wagging competing with the clicking noises Jake's phone made as he typed out a message. Jake put his phone down. "That's common?"

"It used to be." Penelope shrugged. "I did a lot of temping before I started walking dogs. Maybe it's changed." She suspected it hadn't — during her short stint as mayor, she'd been in her office a few times when the janitorial staff had been cleaning the building, and she'd never seen them with more than one trash bin on wheels. "If it makes you feel any better, most of what could possibly be recycled isn't recycled anyhow. Other than cardboard, there's just not much demand for post-consumer recyclables, so they end up in the landfill anyhow."

"Somehow that doesn't really help." He looked at the empty plate in his hand. "I may have to eat another donut to get over this."

"They're not getting any fresher." One of the parishioners owned a donut shop and brought the leftovers to the quilting circle that was held in the church basement every week.

Anything that wasn't eaten by the quilters ended up in CJ's kitchen. CJ had once confessed that he didn't particularly like donuts, so Penelope felt no guilt about eating them.

"I'd be doing CJ a favor by saving him from another stale donut." Jake edged out from under Spot's head and climbed to his feet.

"You'll need the extra calories when you're trying to tire out Brutus this afternoon."

"I'd be more worried about the extra calories if you hadn't eaten most of my first donut."

"See how selfless I am?" She lifted the dog's head so Jake could sit down next to her on the floor again.

Jake's phone buzzed again. "Brian says that you are correct. Or words to that effect."

Penelope looked at him and waited.

"Fine, he said that hundreds of years ago you would have been drowned as a witch. That's how impressed he is."

"Nice attempted save. You tell him that he's going to miss my insights in his new job." She was more worried about Jake now that his closest friend was moving three states away, but she couldn't really say that. Besides, Jake was an outgoing person. He'd handle retirement with his usual ease.

And if he didn't, there was always Esther's list.

*a*s parties went, this one definitely wasn't the worst. People had spread out into all the rooms downstairs, though at least half of them had staked out spots in the kitchen. There was even overflow in the backyard, mostly guests with children, though the night air had turned a little chillier than Penelope had hoped. Nobody was drinking too much, and the little puff pastry cups were the tastiest thing Penelope had eaten in weeks.

Even Brutus, who had a new collar and a clipped-on bow tie for the occasion, was being well-behaved. Mostly. He'd made one toddler cry when she dropped a cracker and he'd eaten it before she could blink, but everyone else in the room had laughed, and Brutus hadn't knocked the girl over in his dash, so Penelope was considering that a win. The only thing that made the evening a little uncomfortable was that all the adults had an eye on the door to see if Chief Purcell would show up.

Everyone knew Jake was retiring earlier than planned, and everyone also knew Chief Purcell was the biggest reason for that. Their leadership styles clashed, they didn't agree on the direction of the department, and worse, though the union leaders backed Purcell, he was an outsider and most of the officers in the department knew and respected Jake. After two months of increasing conflict, it had become clear that if Jake wasn't willing to go to war to get Purcell removed from the position of chief, Jake was going to have to leave. Jake could have found a job with another department, but he'd had enough time in to qualify for retirement, so he'd put in his papers.

So everybody in the house knew Chief Purcell had driven Jake out, but if the chief didn't make an appearance at the retirement party of the assistant chief, that could be seen as an insult. Purcell didn't need to give the officers under him another excuse to dislike him.

Penelope was hoping he didn't show up. She'd spoken to him a few times at occasions where everyone had to be polite and pretend they liked each other, and she'd be happy never to see him again. The man didn't like dogs. Or cats. Or any animals as far as she could tell. That was a bad sign. Plus his teenage son was in a military boarding academy thousands of miles away. Penelope had known parents who chose that option, but she'd also met the children who had gone. There really wasn't anything about Chief Purcell that she liked.

But it had been three hours now, and he hadn't shown up, so people were starting to relax and enjoy themselves.

The real problem, as far as Penelope was concerned, was the number of people who kept congratulating her on the party, as if she'd planned it all and done all the work. The unspoken assumption that, as a woman, Penelope would naturally have been the one who had done everything, despite having her own job, made her jaw ache. She'd brought Brutus outside, ostensibly to give the dog a break from all the people, but really so she could relax her aching neck muscles.

Brian walked up, sparkling water in hand. "You did a great job on the party, Pen."

Penelope took a deep, centering breath. Then she noticed Brian's grin and made a face at him. "Just for that, I should make you listen to the lecture I haven't been giving everyone else."

Brian waved his drink in the direction of the house. "You know at least half the people who have said something have been trying to wind you up, right?"

Penelope had suspected as much. "Give me names and I'll let Brutus slobber all over them." She glanced around the yard to make sure nobody was listening. "If you hear anyone talking about Purcell, can you shut them down? I want Jake to have a good time at his own party, but he's having to spend his time talking people out of making grand gestures of support." The only thing that would accomplish would be to make Jake feel guilty because someone had thrown their career away for no reason.

"Will do." He turned to go back in the house, then stopped. "Just so you know, we're treating Harold Stone's death as suspicious at this point."

"Ha! I knew it wasn't botulism."

"Actually, the pathologist said it might be. She won't know for sure until she runs more tests."

"But…" There had to be more.

"But the initial tests showed his BAC was zero."

"Esther did say he stopped drinking when his kids were still young." Penelope thought about the state of the front garden. "I thought maybe he'd started up again. The front of his house used to be immaculate. No weeds, everything perfectly trimmed. But with the way it looks now, I'd say he hasn't been taking care of it for months."

"And the alcohol fumes were really noticeable when I went inside," Brian agreed. "But we don't get many false negatives with the rapid tests. So if he wasn't drinking, who was spilling vodka all over the room? That isn't some weird alternative to burning incense or smudging, is it?"

It took Penelope a full second to realize that hadn't been a rhetorical question, and then she burst into laughter. "I appreciate your faith that I would know something like that." She shook her head. "No, not that I've ever heard of, anyhow. And even if it was, I *really* doubt an alcoholic who had been sober for decades would choose that."

"So if he wasn't drunk, why didn't he call for help when he started feeling ill? I've looked up the symptoms. He'd have been in a lot of pain for hours." Brian gave a frustrated sigh. "There may still be an innocent explanation. For all I know he killed himself on purpose."

Penelope spent a moment trying to fit all the facts together while she ignored Brutus eating something he'd found on the lawn. "I can see Harold throwing himself in front of a herbicide truck, but I can't see him using botulism as a means of suicide. He worked really hard to convince people they could grow and can their own food. Every time botulism hits the news people stop canning at home. Harold thought everyone should be growing, canning, and freezing all the food they could. He saw the canned food aisle at the grocery store as a sign of a society that was failing."

The steady hum of people talking and laughing inside the house cut off. After a few seconds the sound started again, but it seemed more forced.

Penelope sighed. "I think that's my cue. If I die from the effort of being nice, I'm sorry about the paperwork." She touched Brutus's shoulder to distract him from whatever he was doing. "Let's go, buddy. Time to earn your keep."

"You need me to hang on to him for a while?"

"No, I've got this." Penelope squared her shoulders and walked toward the house. She planned to be an excellent hostess and stick close to Purcell as he made his way around the party. She was betting he'd make his excuses in less than fifteen minutes. Purcell didn't like dogs in general, and Brutus in particular. If he'd been afraid of dogs, Penelope would have had second thoughts about her methods, but he seemed to think dogs were disgusting and people who owned them, weak. He deserved to have Brutus slobber on his leg.

After the cool evening air, the house was warm. There was also more food inside, and Penelope had to force Brutus to keep moving when he wanted to stop where a cluster of guests sat on the sofa, plates held just at the right height for a mastiff to eat without stretching. An equal number of greetings were called out to Penelope and Brutus, but she merely smiled in response and kept moving.

Jake had made it to the door first, and he and Chief Purcell stood in the entryway. Jake had an unopened bottle of wine in one hand, and a determined smile plastered on his face. When he saw Penelope and Brutus arriving, he rubbed his mouth, a sure sign that he was trying to hide a real smile. They may have only been married a few months, but Jake knew her well, and he knew exactly why she had Brutus with her. He turned toward her. "And of course you remember my wife, Penelope."

The chief of police turned as well. "Of course." There was a touch of frost in his tone. "You have a lovely home."

Jake's smile looked more strained, but Penelope wasn't about to waste her time explaining that Jake was more responsible for the decorating than she was. "I think so too." She reached down to adjust Brutus's bow tie. "You've met Brutus before, haven't you?"

"I'd assumed you would have boarded the dog during a function like this."

Brutus burped, an eye-watering mixture that smelled like

salmon and something that had fermented. Penelope patted his head. "No, I think some people only came to play with him. He's far more popular than I am."

The proper thing for a guest to do at that point would be to argue, and she was pretty sure Purcell knew that. "Interesting."

Penelope brightened. If Purcell was actually going to be pleasantly *rude* to her, the whole evening would be a lot more fun. She might even start to like him, against her better judgement. "Jake, can you take Chief Purcell's coat? I'll show him around."

The fact that both men looked a little alarmed was gratifying. Jake recovered first. "Of course." He took the coat and the bottle of wine, and headed toward the guest bedroom.

Penelope tapped Purcell's elbow and guided him toward the dining room. "Can I get you something to drink?" She rattled off the list of what was available, noting that the man must have been around or stepped in something interesting because Brutus was fascinated with his shoes. Penelope nudged Brutus to move a little further away. The shoes looked expensive and uncomfortable, and she didn't trust Purcell not to kick her dog in the guise of protecting his property. Brutus burped again and Penelope reminded herself to keep the bedroom door open so they wouldn't be asphyxiated in their sleep that night. "Your wife couldn't make it this evening?"

"She's out of town." He looked down at Brutus with distaste. "Have you seen Lieutenant Keegan around? I need to talk to him."

"No shop talk during the retirement party," Penelope recited for the fiftieth time that evening. She'd just been talking to Brian about his case, but that was different. They didn't work together. "Everyone needs to practice talking about something other than work for a while."

"Of course *you* would say that. Typical."

"Excuse me?" Pleasantly rude was fun, but this had veered into intentionally offensive territory. What made it more confusing was that Penelope was fairly certain his attack hadn't really been aimed at her.

"Why do you women get hold of a man and then immediately start trying to change him?"

Was it wrong to be flattered by the idea that she could have set her sights on Jake and molded him as she pleased? Penelope suspected that revealed far more vanity than she was comfortable admitting to, but it was a question for later. In the meantime, as much as she didn't like Chief Purcell, she couldn't let him talk like this around his coworkers. "Have it your way. I think Brian's outside."

"You're all the same." The sentence was said under his breath, but the room had gotten quieter and was still audible.

"Ah, yes —" Penelope started to agree.

"I'm sorry, *what* did you say?" Jake was back from hanging up the coat.

"I think..." Penelope said loudly to keep the two men from talking, but with no plan on how to finish the sentence. From the corner of her eye she saw Brutus hunch his shoulders. She knew what was going to happen and decided that it would be the best of her limited options. "... that Brutus may have gotten into something."

With a loud moan, Brutus lowered his head and unleashed a foul-smelling slurry of puff pastry, glitter, carrots, and what had to be the head of a well-decayed squirrel straight onto Chief Purcell's carefully pressed trousers and Italian leather shoes.

CHAPTER 8

*J*n Esther's kitchen the next day, Penelope couldn't stop giggling as she relayed the scene. "A good dry cleaner might be able to salvage the pants, but I think he's going to have to burn those shoes."

"I guess the party was memorable even if it didn't go to plan."

"Are you kidding? It was the best thing that could have happened." Penelope took a sip of lemonade, then regarded the piece of metal in her hand. At the last rose garden raffle, Esther had won a metal sculpture meant to hold multiple pots of succulents. It had arrived as a box of curved struts and bolts, with no instructions other than the picture of the final form. "Instead of having to deal with Purcell acting like an ..." Penelope paused and switched the epithet she was going to use. "... a jerk, we could all pretend to agree that Brutus was the problem and there's a script for what to say when something like that happens. Plus it was the perfect excuse for Purcell to leave right away." Penelope snorted again as she remembered the silence that had followed, broken only by the sound of slime dripping onto the floor. "If

I could figure out how to teach Brutus to do that on command, I would. It was well worth whatever it's going to cost to replace those shoes."

There was a knock on the front door, and Esther put down the metal pieces she was trying to fit together and went to answer it.

"I think his wife might have left him," Penelope said to Esther's retreating back. She squinted at the picture, and tried to fit two more pieces together. The bolt holes didn't line up.

"That would explain why she took so much luggage with her on what was supposed to be a one week trip," Esther called back. "It didn't fit in the trunk of the cab that took her to the airport."

Penelope grinned as she picked up another piece to try. Someday she was going to tell Esther something the other woman didn't already know, but today was not that day.

Esther came back into the kitchen with the young man Penelope had seen leaving a couple of days ago. Harold's son, Bear — no, wait, he went by Edward now, Penelope reminded herself — had been a few grades behind her own son, which meant he must be close to thirty, but he had retained something of the uncertain little boy about him. Still, he'd lost his father recently, and that could throw even the most mature adult off balance. She stood up to greet him.

Esther moved to her position and picked up the pitcher to pour another glass. "Edward, this is my friend Penelope Standing. Her son Seth was three or four years ahead of you in school."

"I'm so sorry for your loss," Penelope said.

"Thank you." Edward had the look of someone who was waiting for the next assault, and she wondered what people had been saying to him. From past experience she suspected it was something like *Your father was not my*

41

favorite person, but... Family relationships could be difficult, and Edward deserved to be able to grieve, or not, without being forced to defend his father's memory or pretend he had been a person he hadn't been. A line formed between his brows as they sat down. "You're the person who found him."

"Yes."

"But I thought he was found by the mail carrier. Aren't you the mayor?"

Small town politics had started to make more sense when she had realized half the voters never found out who had won the most recent election. "I was, but not any more. Now I run my pet sitting business and occasionally deliver mail when needed."

"Oh. That makes sense." He gazed at all the metal pieces on the table, then glanced up at her. "Sorry, that seems like a weird thing to say, I know. It's just that so much of this *doesn't* make sense."

"Which makes it seem unreal." Penelope nodded. Sudden death had felt that way to her as well.

"Yes! That's it!" He looked at the picture in front of Penelope, then picked up two pieces and inserted the bolts into the pre-drilled holes, fastening nuts loosely on the back. He picked up another piece and lined it up.

Penelope and Esther looked at each other. They had unpacked the box nearly an hour before and hadn't found two pieces that fit together in the time since. They quietly put down the pieces they'd been holding and waited.

Edward hadn't noticed their look. He picked up another piece and added it. "It seems like it can't be real because it's like everything was set up as a story but then we never got to hear the end of it." His hands stilled.

Esther looked like she was holding her breath. Penelope ventured a question, hoping he hadn't reached the end of his miraculous ability to assemble the thing in front of them. "In what way?"

Edward glanced up at her, then back down at the table. He picked up another piece and fit it onto his structure. Esther started breathing again. "We were all supposed to get together that day... the day you found him... for a family meeting." His fingers stilled.

Esther frowned at Penelope. Penelope decided she'd been tasked to keep him talking until the thing, which could loosely be described as a porcupine with loops to hold tiny pots instead of spines, was assembled. "Did your family often have meetings?"

"Not lately. Or, I guess I should say, not that I was invited to." He paused to look at the picture again, then dug through the pile of metal until he found the one he wanted. To Penelope it looked like every other piece, and she wanted to ask him why he'd chosen it, but if she disrupted his concentration and this thing didn't get put together, Esther might serve her lemonade without sugar for the next year. "We'd only started talking again a few months ago."

Penelope remembered his history of addiction. "At least you were able to mend some fences before he died."

"I guess... Except the last time I saw him we got in this huge fight." He frowned, as if the memory puzzled him, and his hands stilled.

Penelope wondered which of Dante's levels of hell was reserved for people who asked questions to a newly bereaved son just so they could get a garden sculpture assembled. Clearly she and Esther were destined for that place. She only hoped the person who had decided to send a box full of unlabeled metal was in some level below them. "A fight about the usual things, or something new?"

"About the usual things, but it didn't make any sense." His hands started moving again. "He accused me of stealing his pills." He sighed. "I did steal a lot of things — from him and everyone else — but not since I stopped using. I guess I can't really blame him for not believing me when I said I hadn't." He dug through the pieces again. "Pills, though. Since when had my father taken pills? You knew him, right?"

"A bit."

Edward grinned ruefully at her, then looked down at his hands again. "You didn't have to know my father very well to know how he felt about modern medicine. He smoked weed if he had a headache, or his joints were acting up, but that was it."

The main ring of the porcupine's body was nearly together. "Did you ask him about it?"

"I didn't get a chance. We had started having lunch together once a week. That was about as often as we could be in the same room without irritating each other. Everything seemed fine when I got there. We made lunch together like we always did. Then he went to the bathroom and when he came back he just started yelling at me." Edward's face flushed. "He said some things, and then I didn't even care that it made no sense and we were just screaming at each other."

"What day was that?"

"Two... no, three days ago. The day before you found him. I finally decided I needed to leave before I said something I'd regret. Well, regret more than the things I'd already said, I guess. I thought I'd see him at the family meeting the next day and try to convince him that I hadn't done anything."

"Were the family meetings usually about the business or about personal things?" The pieces Penelope had been convinced were part of the feet had been assembled into the porcupine's ears. She and Esther would never have put the thing together, not even if they'd spent the whole day trying.

"My dad wasn't very good about separating the two. My sister runs the shop, and my mom still handles the publishing even though they've been divorced for years. I was the only one who wasn't part of the business."

"That must have been hard."

"Yes, but... I'm not saying that I went about it the right way, but I think it was good that I put some space between me and my family for a few years. When I came back, my dad tried to get me to take over some of the canning classes since Skye hates canning and he was tired of teaching people. I think that was the first time I ever really said no to him." He bolted the head onto the body. "I thought he was going to be really upset about it, but he wasn't." He paused and frowned. "I thought it was just a sign that he had given up on me, but I think maybe he was starting to give up on the business. When he set up the meeting this week, I thought he was going to tell us he was planning to retire." He gave a humorless laugh. "Skye thought he was going to announce he was going to rehab."

Penelope's curiosity got the better of her. "*Had* he started drinking again?" Esther gave her a conflicted look. On the one hand, the question really was rude, especially since it was about someone who had just died, and no matter how much Esther needed to find out information, she was always kind. On the other hand, Edward had finished the body and started attaching the spines, all of which were nearly identical except for the tilt. Penelope and Esther *might* be able to finish putting the porcupine together, but Penelope didn't want to chance it.

Edward threaded another bolt. "I don't know." He picked up two metallic spines and lined them up. "I know *something* had changed in the last few months. A couple of times when I went over for lunch the sink was full of dishes, like he hadn't cleaned anything since the last time I was there. If you knew my dad... That was really unusual." He made a decision on the pieces in his hands and affixed the first one. "I never saw him drinking, and he never seemed drunk to me, but addicts can be good at hiding that sort of thing, you know?"

"It looked like he hadn't been gardening as much."

"If I hadn't fixed his automatic watering system a couple weeks ago, everything would have died. He hadn't even noticed it wasn't running. And Skye said he kept showing up late at the shop, and cancelling classes at the last minute." He picked up the final pieces and started threading them into place. "She was always a lot closer to him than I was. She's probably right. It's just weird that I never saw anything at the house."

Edward finished attaching the last piece. He pushed at the sculpture, controlling its wobble. "If you have a wrench, I can tighten these down so it's more sturdy." He suddenly looked up in alarm. "Oh. Did I just finish the puzzle you were working on? Hang on, I can take it back apart."

Esther grabbed his arm so fast she almost fell out of her wheelchair. She straightened, and then patted his hand. "No, no, it's fine."

Penelope stood up. She'd been in Esther's house enough to know where everything was stored. "Let me get you a wrench."

CHAPTER 9

The pastries from the party weren't quite as fresh the next day, but they were still tasty, and there were enough vegetables to go along with them to provide a satisfying lunch. "If that young man ever decides to start a business assembling things, he'll make a fortune," Penelope said to Jake as she finished relaying her visit with Esther and Edward. "I know at least three people with furniture that's still sitting in a box because they can't figure out how it's supposed to go together."

"If they want help, let me know. I'll carve out some time in my packed schedule."

Penelope raised an eyebrow at him. "Seems like you've been pretty busy so far." From the looks of things, Jake had spent most of the morning cleaning up from the party. The caterers had wiped down everything when they had picked up the tables and the dishes after the party, but now the kitchen floor gleamed and the carpet had vacuum lines in it.

Jake nodded. "I signed Brutus up for a class. I think he gets bored without anything to do."

Penelope put some effort into not choking on the food

she'd just chewed. "You think... Brutus might be bored." Loud snores emanated from the living room where the dog in question had gone after it became clear she wasn't going to feed him again. "I'm skeptical, but another obedience class certainly couldn't hurt."

Jake huffed a laugh. "It probably wouldn't help all that much either. Have you met our dog?" He put more vegetables and dip on his plate. "No, I signed him up for scent tracking class. It sounded interesting."

Penelope tried to imagine Brutus expending the effort to follow a scent through difficult terrain and failed. "I think you'll be lucky if he tracks anything other than somebody's lunch, but you're right. It does sound interesting." A minute change in Jake's expression tipped her off that he hadn't told her everything. "What happened?"

"I took him with me when I went to sign up, and he ate the supplies on the way home." He paused to acknowledge her laugh. "It's okay. It was nothing toxic. But do you know where to buy essential oils? If I order them online they might not get here in time."

Penelope could think of at least three places in town that sold them, a result of the aromatherapy movement that was still popular, but only one of those places was somewhere she wanted to go. "Homespun Harold's should have them. I can pick some up for you this afternoon if you want. I'll be going right by there."

Jake didn't even try to hide his amusement. "Ah, yes, a selfless act that just happens to take you to the one place you wanted to snoop around in the first place."

"You say snoop, but I say supporting a member of the community who has suffered a tragic loss."

"Because you don't believe the tragic loss was what it appeared to be."

Penelope allowed that point. "I just don't believe he accidentally gave himself botulism. He knew what he was doing. And even if he did somehow manage to eat spoiled food without noticing it, why didn't he call for help? He wasn't drunk." Something that had been poking at the back of her mind suddenly fell into place. "In fact, I'm one hundred percent positive he didn't eat from a spoiled jar."

"Because…?"

"Because Crunch is still alive."

Jake frowned in confusion. "Who is Crunch?"

"Harold's dog. Crunch ate everything Harold did." Penelope saw his gaze move toward the living room. "And not like your dog eats everything we do because he keeps getting into things. Harold didn't trust any of the companies that made dog food because they might put fillers or something unnatural in there. He always fed Crunch the same things he ate." She'd heard Harold proselytizing at the dog park enough to know how it worked. "He would make his meal, and then he would literally split it onto two plates and give one of them to Crunch. I saw him do it when I was in the shop once. If Harold ate spoiled food, why wasn't Crunch sick too?"

Jake looked up at the ceiling for a few moments in his normal thinking pose. Finally, he looked back at her. "We need to talk to Brian about this."

Penelope nodded. "I'll let you call him. I need to go buy some essential oils."

* * *

HOMESPUN HAROLD'S ALL-NATURAL EMPORIUM SOLD AN image of a simple lifestyle where every moment was carefree and the stress of modern life was washed away. In reality, the simple lifestyle turned out to have a lot of conflicting smells and came with an inflated price tag. Living without stress required a lot of resources.

The shop had changed since the last time Penelope had been there, with the canning jars and bulk food bins that had been most of the store now relegated to one corner. Woven ponchos were artfully draped over scarecrows made from stalks of corn, and individually-wrapped bars of colorful soap were displayed on quaint fruit baskets that had never been near an apple in their entire existence. Aside from the one corner, Penelope might not have recognized it as the same store, but there was still an underlying smell of patchouli.

A chalkboard on a tripod near the front doors advertised upcoming classes. Imperfectly erased letters told her that the canning class had recently been replaced by another hand spinning class. The price made her widen her eyes. Making your own yarn was an activity for people with more money than she ever made, even if the participants did end up with a bag of wool and a drop spindle at the end of the session. She was aware the global economy devalued goods by exploiting poor people, but it still seemed excessive to pay more than the price of her first car for a one hour class and enough wool to make a pot-holder.

Other classes taught how to color the wool using all-natural dyes, and simple crochet techniques. Or you could use your yarn to weave a basket out of locally-sourced pine needles. The sample basket, small enough to fit in her hand and having just enough imperfections to be attractive, was nice, but Penelope couldn't imagine what she would use it for, other than to sit on a shelf and collect dust until Brutus ate it. Jake probably wouldn't appreciate her mortgaging the house to pay for it, either.

Then she noticed the asterisk on the pricing. As with new cars, apparently only the uninformed paid full price. Home-spun Harold's had gone to a subscription model; for a modest monthly charge, patrons would get a hefty discount on classes, not including the cost of materials, and also got a chance to sign up before the registration was open to the general public. Penelope did some rough calculations in her head. If the subscriber took one class every couple months, it was still a deal, assuming one had a burning desire to make pine baskets from scratch.

"Are you interested in signing up for one of the classes?" Skye had come forward while Penelope had been busy doing the math. "We still have a couple slots in the next cold press soap class, and it's steeply discounted." Her voice trailed off. "I know you. You were there at my father's house. Penny?"

Skye definitely fit in the newer section of the store more than in the granola corner. Everything about her seemed simple, but it was deceptive. With the eye of someone who had spent most of her life on a strict budget, Penelope could recognize an expensive haircut and color, clothes designed for her frame, and shoes that managed to appear clunky and yet somehow graceful at the same time. Even her hands showed signs of a fresh manicure and clear varnish. To people who didn't look too closely, Skye would appear to be the perfect example of a natural lifestyle, without anything like dry skin or split ends that might scare them off. Penelope admired how Skye had put the image together, even if she could see through it.

"Penelope. I'm so sorry for your loss." She was fairly certain she'd said that before, but it never hurt to repeat it.

"Thank you. Were you interested in signing up for a class, or did you need something else?"

The difference between father and daughter was striking. By this point Harold would have been launching into one of his rants about the evils of unnatural food with selected examples culled from decades of industry exposés. Cancer, arthritis, and obesity all resulted from GMOs and chemicals, according to Harold. Coming into the shop when Harold had been in charge had always been an experience, though not always a pleasant one.

Shopping while Skye was in charge felt like the transaction that it was.

"I'm really here for some essential oils. Something nontoxic, in case the dog eats it," she hastened to add.

Skye's lips tightened into a brief smile. "Of course. Let me show you what we have." She threaded between the aisles to a display near the window. Tiny vials were arranged on tufts of wool in straw baskets. "You're in luck. I was just teaching classes on distilling essential oils last week, so these are all fresh."

They were all very pricey, too, but Penelope had been prepared for that. She chose two of the least expensive, lemon and peppermint, plus a vial of something called *Harold's Own* because it seemed like the right thing to do, and smiled at Skye. "I think this should be it." If Skye had been a dog person, Penelope would have told her what they would be used for, and they might have talked a bit, but Skye didn't seem to be at all interested.

Skye led her to a counter with a tablet connected to a credit card reader.

Penelope tried again while Skye tapped on the screen. "Things have certainly changed here. I remember the first time I came in. Your dad was writing all the sales in a ledger."

Skye pushed the screen forward so Penelope could read it. "Here's your total. Will that be credit?"

Penelope paused in handing over her credit card. There was something about Skye that made her curious. "How much was that soap making class?"

CHAPTER 10

"Soap." Jake's voice was noncommittal as he looked at the instruction sheet in front of him. They were seated at the picnic table in the backyard, with Brutus locked safely inside the house. Jake was wearing a pair of too-large rubber gloves and had arrayed all the scent-tracking supplies in front of him. "You signed up for a class on how to make soap."

"I almost signed you up for it, too, but I figured one of us is probably enough. I can teach you what I learn if you're interested." She watched him struggle to open the tiny vial obscured by the loose tips of the gloves, then reached forward and took it from him. The smell of lemons filled the air. "I'll be able to give it away as Christmas presents for people we either love or hate, depending on how it turns out."

"Very practical." Jake put a cotton ball over the top of the vial, inverted it briefly, and dropped the cotton into a pre-labeled sealable sandwich bag. "I take it that Harold's daughter did not immediately tell you everything you wanted to know?" He repeated the process with the next cotton ball and bag.

"Maybe I just wanted to learn how to make soap." Penelope took the bags that had cotton balls in them, sealed them, and set them to the side. Brutus had his head against the glass door, watching them closely while a puddle of drool pooled beneath him. "The shop has really changed since the last time I went in there. Though I guess that's been a few years."

"A few years in real time, or a few years in our time?"

"I needed some chia seeds for something, and it was before the grocery stores started carrying them." Penelope closed a few more bags as she thought about it. Her son had wanted to make a chia pet out of a clay bust he'd created in art class. "Probably at least fifteen years. I guess it's been more than a few."

Smart man that he was, Jake didn't react to that other than a twitch of his lips. He switched to the vial labeled *Harold's Own* which turned out to be an odd combination that reminded Penelope of pulling weeds on a hot day.

"Harold used to sell to the health nuts. Skye seems to have changed it to fleece the bored yoga crowd." She told him about the classes and the items available for sale.

"You said it yourself — the grocery store didn't used to carry chia seeds. Now there's an entire aisle of natural food. If the store hadn't changed, it probably would have gone out of business."

"Maybe. I still wonder how much of the change was in the last few months. Something was different with him." She recapped the vial that he handed her, and opened another one. Mint replaced the smell of weeds.

"People do fall off the wagon, you know, even after decades."

"I guess." She thought about the last few times she'd seen Harold. "But he was at the dog park with Crunch in the early evening a few times a week. And he seemed okay then." He certainly hadn't driven as if he'd been drinking.

"Some people hide it really well." He continued dabbing mint oil onto cotton balls.

"Except..." Penelope considered how to articulate her thoughts as she sealed more plastic bags. "We seem to be using the evidence to say two different things at the same time. 'He was drinking so much that he was missing work and not taking care of his garden', but also 'He was so good at hiding his drinking that nobody ever suspected it'. I don't think they can both be true."

The smell of mint had started to become cloying by the time Jake handed over the vial to be recapped. He pulled off the bulky gloves and started sealing the bagged cotton balls into a second bag. "Maybe it wasn't alcohol. Maybe he was sick. Or depressed."

"That would fit. But Skye would have known if he was that sick."

"Unless he was hiding it from her. Or hiding it from himself. You said that he preached that natural foods cured everything. What would he have done if he'd gotten seriously ill with something like cancer? Would he have gone for treatment, or would he have just hidden the symptoms until he couldn't keep it a secret anymore?"

"Surely he would have..." Penelope stopped. "No, you're right. It's possible he would have just assumed he would heal on his own." She got distracted by the tackle box he had started loading the supplies into. "Since when have you fished?"

"Never. Why? Oh, this?" He nodded his head at the tackle box. "They were on sale at the hardware store a while back. I figured I would need it someday for something. I think it's sturdy enough that Brutus can't break into it."

A long drawn out moan came from the other side of the

glass door. Penelope buried her face in her hands as Jake started laughing loudly. They both knew that sound. Brutus did not like to be excluded from anything, and the first time they had closed the bedroom door with him on the other side, his overwrought moaning had left them both laughing so hard they couldn't breathe. Penelope had partially bridged the gap between spontaneity and listening to the dog howl by keeping a stash of treat-filled dog toys in the freezer.

Jake finished stowing the supplies and latched the lid. "So... You busy this afternoon?" The studied casualness of his voice would have alerted Penelope to his intentions even if Brutus hadn't taken a breath to start another howl. They were both smiling when their eyes met.

Penelope checked the time. "I don't have to be anywhere for an hour." Heidi, the German Shepherd she took for a jog every day, wouldn't mind if she was a little late. "You find somewhere safe for that, and I'll deal with your dog. Meet you upstairs in two minutes."

They ran toward the house.

CHAPTER 11

*H*eidi had indeed forgiven her for being half an hour late, especially when Penelope let her choose the pace. The German Shepherd was a big fan of sprinting across the grass field at the high school. As a result, Penelope was feeling pleasantly tired when she finished with her other pet sitting clients, and was ready for a long bath, dinner, and an evening of dozing on the couch.

Brian's car was parked in front of the house, which instantly reordered Penelope's priorities. The long bath could wait. Brian would have information about Harold, and if it wasn't too sensitive, he might be willing to tell her about it.

The two men were in the kitchen, Jake chopping onions at the counter while Brian sat at the table with a beer. "Jake told me about Harold's dog," Brian said, after they'd greeted each other.

"Good." She dug the latest checks and invoices out of her backpack and shoved them on top of the others in the folder meant for that purpose.

Brian watched the process in disbelief. "I think you

should let Jake become the pet sitting accountant. Maybe go paperless."

The idea matched so closely with something Jake had said a few days before that Penelope glared at her husband. Jake held up his hands in surrender. "I didn't say anything. I swear." A piece of onion fell off the knife onto the floor. Brutus abruptly stopped snoring in the living room and ran into the kitchen to grab it before Jake had finished leaning over to pick it up.

"At least we know his ears are fine. Did Jake tell you he's training Brutus to become a scent tracking dog?"

Brian's gaze drifted toward the living room where the couch creaked as Brutus got comfortable again. "I've met tracking dogs. They seemed to be more... driven."

"Hey, now, don't be disparaging our dog," Jake said over the sizzle of onions coming into contact with hot oil. "He has all kinds of drive."

"You'll be lucky if he doesn't eat whatever has the scent you're supposed to be tracking."

Penelope studied a spot on the ceiling so she didn't have to meet Brian's eyes.

"You're kidding." Brian snorted. "Well, I've heard it's good for old people to have hobbies when they retire. Did you know the Italians have a word for men who gather around outside construction sites to tell each other what the workers are doing wrong? I can't remember what it is, but it exists."

"Ha! I was just talking about that with Esther. But Jake would never stay outside."

"I don't know anything about construction." Jake shook the spatula at them. "Just you wait, though. Someday there's going to be a lost child with a bag of crackers, and you won't be laughing at my dog then, will you?" Another bit of onion fell off the spatula and Brutus raced through the kitchen again.

Penelope left them laughing and went to go clean up.

* * *

SHE MANAGED TO REIN IN HER CURIOSITY ABOUT HAROLD'S death all through dinner as they discussed Brian's impending move. Initially she'd been skeptical when she'd heard he'd taken a job heading up the cyber security section at a telecommunications company — she'd seen the desktop on his workstation and he still relied on programs that were no longer being sold because he didn't like to use a mouse if he didn't have to — but he'd explained that they had people for the technical work. They needed someone who knew what evidence was useful and how to preserve it. Penelope was fairly certain the main reason he'd taken the job was to put some space between himself and his soon-to-be ex-wife, but Brian seemed to be excited about the new challenge.

Brian was drying the dishes as Penelope washed them, and she tried to figure out a casual way to ask if there was any new information. She'd thought up and discarded three different attempts before Jake started laughing at the kitchen table where he was sitting.

"Just tell her before she hurts herself."

Brian handed the plate he was drying back to her. "You missed a spot. There was a jar of asparagus in the refriger-ator that had all kinds of botulism spores in it, but —" he quickly added when she took a breath to dispute his claim. "But there weren't any fingerprints on the jar."

"None at all?"

"Nope, it had been wiped clean. All the other jars were covered with Stone's fingerprints, so it's officially considered a homicide."

"There go the department's quarterly stats," Jake grumbled. Then he brightened. "But I don't have to present them to the city council any more, so I don't care."

"So what happens now?"

"We're re-interviewing all the neighbors, and tracking down everyone with a grudge. That may take a year or two. He rubbed a lot of people the wrong way."

Penelope rinsed the plate again and handed it back. "Does that mean I get to be a suspect?"

"Sorry. I think you're so far down the list that unless it turns out that there's another will leaving everything to you, you're off the hook."

The pan that Jake had used for the sauce had tomato paste burned onto the rim, giving her an excuse not to talk while she wrestled with her conscience about passing along what Edward had said. "Just so you know, Harold and his son apparently got into a big argument that day."

"As confirmed by the neighbors on both sides and Bear himself."

That made her feel better. "I don't think he did it. And he goes by his middle name, Edward, now." She rinsed the pan and handed it to him.

Brian handed it right back. "You missed a spot."

"To poison someone with botulism, you'd have to plan it weeks or months in advance. Edward couldn't have just gotten angry and done it that day."

"No, but he could have gotten angry and decided that it was the perfect time to do something he'd prepared for. Bear... Edward would know how to can something improperly, he didn't get along with his father, and even though he doesn't gain directly, his mother does, and I'm fairly certain his mother is more likely to give him money than his father would have been. Plus he admits that they ate what might have been Harold's last meal together."

Penelope rinsed the pot again. "I'm not buying it. They ate

lunch together before the fight, so it doesn't make sense to use that argument as a sign of motive. And half the town knows how *not* to can things. Harold taught classes. Plus I would imagine there's a pretty large overlap between those people and people who didn't get along with him."

Brian examined the pot closely, and then finally started drying it. "This case has more potential suspects than you can shake a stick at. And the alibis aren't helping things. His ex-wife was alone at home; her current husband was out of town on a business trip. Stone's son was also home alone; his girlfriend was staying at her parents' that night. His daughter is the only one who has any proof of where she was. She was rearranging things at the shop all night, and we have security footage of her going in with, wait for it…"

"Fast food?"

"Yes, indeed. You can actually see the grease coming through the bag. She didn't leave until late morning right before she showed up at his place. Then there's the rest of the people who hated him. I swear half of them are hoping to get charged with murder just for the bragging rights."

"You met Harold. What did you expect? And what's with the place smelling like alcohol? If Harold really wasn't drinking again, that means someone came back when he was dead or dying to set the scene. I might be able to poison Jake someday so I can get all his money, but I don't think I could hang around while he died."

Jake looked up when he heard his name. "Thank you?"

"I'm just saying that I can't see Edward doing that."

"And you've known this guy how long?" Brian timed his question carefully so she would hear him over the clattering of the other dishes as he put the dry pot in the cabinet.

"Edward? Only twenty minutes or so. But Esther has known him since he was a little kid."

"People change, Pen. And Harold Stone might have been

the one to spill the alcohol. He could have dropped a bottle. Everyone says he was still sober, but there were three bottles of vodka in with his canning supplies. To me that says he was secretly drinking."

"That's because you don't grow your own herbs." Penelope rinsed her hands off and opened the cupboard door in the corner of the kitchen. Because of the way the cabinets had been put together, it opened to a long narrow space. She pulled out a jar with mint stems surrounded by a dark green liquid, and a half-used bottle of inexpensive vodka. "Mint extract. It needs another week or two before I take out the mint and filter the liquid."

Brian took the jar from her and looked at it. "You're kidding."

"Where did you think it came from? Alcohol is used in most extracts, and filtered vodka is perfect for the purpose. Harold sold a bunch of different extracts in his store. It would surprise me more if you *hadn't* found vodka with his supplies."

"It's always the things you don't know anything about that come back to bite you." Brian sighed. "Would you do me a favor? Can you look over the photos of the house and tell me if anything strikes you as wrong? If you really need to go inside the house, I'd have to make it official and then Purcell might be a problem, but the photographer documented everything in the kitchen."

Penelope tried to keep the eagerness out of her voice. "I guess. I mean, if you think it might help."

* * *

LOOKING THROUGH PHOTOGRAPHS OF HIPPIE HAROLD'S kitchen confirmed a few things for Penelope. First, no matter what else was going on with him, he hadn't slipped in his canning and storage. She coveted the walk-in pantry with floor to ceiling shelves, custom-made to allow room for one row of jars with a small gap at the top. Each shelf was labeled with the month and year, and each jar had a label indicating the contents and the date it had been canned. Based on the shelves, he had canned less in the last few months, but those jars didn't look any different from the older ones.

Large jars of lemon, mint, and vanilla extract were in progress on a shelf near the floor, along with extracts of some other herbs that Penelope couldn't quite make out the labels for. The bottles of vodka were in a different area of the kitchen, along with cases of new Ball jars, and something that looked like equipment from a chemistry lab which she thought might be used to make essential oils. She wasn't surprised nobody had figured out the purpose of the vodka if they didn't know about extracts. It really did look like the perfect place for an alcoholic to hide his stash.

The rest of the kitchen held the usual items, though Harold ate nothing that came pre-made, so he had well-used canisters of flour, various grains, sugar, and salt on the counter. It looked like he had made his own pasta and bread. A wooden egg holder with seven of the cavities occupied took up the space between the flour and salt canisters.

Brian interrupted her as she was ready to click to the next picture. "Why wouldn't he be keeping his eggs in the refrigerator?"

"Because he wasn't buying them from the store. He probably bought them at the farmer's market, or from someone who kept chickens at home. I think it has something to do with how much the eggs are washed."

She kept scrolling. Nothing in the rest of the cupboards or on the counters particularly surprised her. He had seemed to prefer unscented homemade cleaning products, and as she'd expected, there was nothing in the house that looked like it had been made or purchased specifically for his dog.

A bucket with a lid fastened by a clamp held food scraps, vegetable ends, and egg shells. Harold also had a tall silver bin, with side by side trash and recycling. "Ooh, Jake, he had your Swedish stainless steel trash can." The lid opened automatically when you waved a hand over the sensor. Jake had spent a few days lusting after the same version online.

"Must be nice to have a dog that respects boundaries," Jake called from the living room where he was currently buried under Brutus while he scratched the dog's belly. The bin had been out of his intended price range, but the coolness factor had almost won him over. He might have bought it if Penelope hadn't pointed out that if they could wave a hand and have it open automatically, Brutus would also be able to make it open. Since the whole reason Jake was looking at trash cans was to Brutus-proof the kitchen, that had made him close the browser tab with a heavy sigh.

In Harold's case, the recycling side had been completely full, and the trash nearly empty. Another photo showed the contents of each side spread out on plastic. The recycling held about what she expected. Cardboard, newspapers, a few plastic tubs, and a fair amount of junk mail. Penelope had probably delivered some of it. The trash barely covered any of the plastic used as a background for the photo, with just a few stickers of the type found on fruit, and an empty bottle of the same vodka found with the canning supplies.

"That proves it." Penelope stabbed a finger at the laptop screen. "Somebody else was there."

Brian leaned over to look at what she was pointing at. "The only fingerprints on that bottle were his and the liquor store clerk's. And she has been out of the country for two weeks."

"Harold would never have put a glass bottle in the trash.

Never." She'd once seen him nearly come to blows with another man at the dog park over it.

"The recycling side was full. Maybe he wasn't feeling well enough to empty it right then. Most glass ends up in the landfill anyhow."

"Trust me. If Harold could make it to the kitchen to put the bottle in the recycling, he never would have put it in the trash."

Brian closed the laptop. "I thought this was going to be a simple unattended death and now I'm going to have to explain canning and herbal extracts to someone when I hand the case off. Has anyone ever told you that you complicate things?"

In the living room, Jake laughed.

CHAPTER 12

The porcupine sculpture stood proudly in the middle of Esther's front garden, the tiny pots at the end of the spines waiting to be filled, but when Penelope stopped by in the afternoon, planting succulents was the last thing on Esther's mind.

"They've taken Edward in for questioning." Esther was paging through her address book, a tattered thing with pages falling out and business cards taped in. "I need to find him a lawyer. Amelia would never think to get him one."

The only time Penelope's son had needed a lawyer, after a prank had gone wrong due to an excess of enthusiasm and a lack of common sense, Seth had hired his own counsel before Penelope had even found out he'd been arrested. "It's probably a good idea to check, but I'm pretty sure Edward knows some criminal lawyers. Doesn't he have some convictions?"

Esther paused. "His fiancée would probably know, wouldn't she?" She went back to paging through her address book, while Penelope went back down the hall to scoop out the litter boxes with three cats supervising. Once she was out of sight, Penelope texted her husband. *Edward in custody. Does he have a lawyer yet? Esther is worried.* Jake would know who to ask.

The cats circled as she scooped, playing a feline game of musical chairs — the prize was to be the first cat to use the freshly-cleaned litter box. This time the winner was Pirate, who didn't let three legs and one eye slow him down. Penelope cleaned the other boxes, then did a second round of scooping after all the cats were finished. She had just finished sweeping litter off the floor when her phone buzzed. *Hammerhead is in the room making sure he keeps his mouth shut. Tell Esther not to worry.*

"Hammerhead" was the nickname everyone used for Vivica Hammer, at least when the lawyer wasn't in the room. Penelope had never met her, but she'd heard enough about her to feel better about Edward's situation. She wondered who was footing the bill. Hammer wasn't cheap, and Edward hadn't looked like he had many resources.

Penelope went back out to the kitchen and washed her hands. Esther was on the landline, scrawling a new entry in the address book. "Thank you. I'll let you know."

Esther hung up and Penelope cut in before she could start dialing again. "Jake says that Vivica Hammer is already representing him. She's good. Expensive, but good."

Esther placed the handset back in the cradle. "I just found out why he could afford a good lawyer. His fiancée is the daughter of Rebecca Wallingstone. I met her once, and I had no idea. She teaches high school students."

Rebecca Wallingstone had been an actress in her younger years, and had been realistic enough to know that her talent would elevate her, but choosing a few roles that required nudity would take her further. She'd been a tabloid favorite for a few years, as she paired up with a string of well-known actors, so it was somewhat of a shock to the public when she revealed that she'd been saving and investing her money wisely the entire time. She had married a movie producer and retired at thirty, and from all accounts had been perfectly happy in the years since, raising their children and running a winery.

"I wonder if his girlfriend — " The absurdity of knowing a person only in relation to someone else irritated Penelope. "What is her name? I refuse to keep calling her Edward's fiancée."

"Tweetie." For the first time since Penelope had come over, there was humor in Esther's eyes.

Penelope blinked. "Really?"

"That's how she was introduced to me. I suspect it's not her legal name, but you never know, do you?"

Penelope nodded. "Anyhow, I wonder if Tweetie —" She almost made it without stumbling over the name. "I wonder if she has money of her own, or if there was an emergency call home to get help to pay for a lawyer."

"Why would that..." Esther's question trailed off. "Of course. If she has her own money, that removes the financial incentive. Did Harold have much to leave?"

"I'm not sure. He hadn't been paying his bills, but I think that might have been a symptom of something else. The shop here in town is tiny, but he licensed the Homespun Harold name years ago and it did really well in... Spain? Portugal? One of those countries. Plus I think the publishing company is doing okay. That one yoga book is still all over the place." None of that proved that Harold didn't have debts greater than his assets, but Brian *had* mentioned money as a motive.

Esther went back to paging through her address book. "I'll do my best to find out if Tweetie has money or if they're just living on their salaries. I'm glad he has a good lawyer, but I'd be happier if the detectives spent their time looking at a *real* suspect."

CHAPTER 13

*T*he warm afternoon had slipped into a comfortable evening, though the mosquitos were out, making Penelope wish she'd put on something with longer sleeves. She thought about dashing back into the house, but watching Jake and Brutus together was too entertaining. Also, she had the important job of holding the extra treats.

"Okay, treats in one hand, scent cue in the other." Jake talked himself through the process again, as if making sure he hadn't skipped any steps. "Then I hold my hands two feet apart." He suited action to words.

What was *supposed* to happen at this point was that Brutus would sniff each hand, and the minute he sniffed the hand with the scent cue, Jake would bring the other hand over and let him have the treat. Brutus had done it perfectly on the first try. Every attempt to repeat the process had been a different disaster.

This time Brutus started with a play bow, then rushed around behind Jake and barreled into the back of his knees. Jake landed flat on his back, and both treat and scent cue went flying.

Penelope put a foot on the treat and snatched the baggie with the lemon-scented cotton ball off the ground before Brutus could get to either one of them. "No treats for bad dogs," she explained to Brutus as he tried to push her foot out of the way with his nose. "You okay over there?"

Jake seemed to be having trouble sitting up, but she was relieved to see it was because he was laughing. "This dog."

"He really does seem to like this new game you've made up." When Brutus went over to lick Jake's face, Penelope took the opportunity to retrieve the treat under her foot. It came away with a bit of mud, but she didn't think a dog that ate decayed woodland creatures would mind all that much. "Alright, Mr. Bad Dog, come over here and let your chew toy get off the ground."

In the time it took Jake to stand up and brush himself off, she and Brutus had successfully done the exercise three times.

Jake narrowed his eyes at her. "How did you do that?"

"It's all in the timing." Decades of owning her own and dealing with other people's pets had given her an edge. "Plus, this isn't the spot where I wrestle with him every evening."

"Oh." After a moment Jake raised one eyebrow. "Were you planning on mentioning that, or were you just going to keep watching?"

"The two of you seemed to be having fun." She smiled. "But if you're done rolling around with him, why don't we move to the front yard and try it again?"

While Jake was putting Brutus's leash on, Penelope grabbed a sweatshirt to thwart the mosquitos.

The front yard had more distractions in the way of people and other dogs walking by, but despite that, Brutus and Jake were able to successfully complete the first exercise three times. Then it was time for Jake to randomly switch hands for the treat and scent cue, which threw Brutus off a bit the first time.

Brian drove up right as they were finishing.

"Jake's working on training Brutus for scent tracking," Penelope explained when Brian finished greeting the dog.

Brian looked Jake over and removed a bit of grass from his shoulder. "Are you playing the part of the corpse he's supposed to find?"

"I think that might be the advanced class."

Brian shook his head and turned back to Penelope. "Just thought I'd let you know that your friend Edward is back home again."

"Because of his lawyer, or because you believe he didn't do it?"

Brian's carefully controlled expression didn't give anything away, but that was how Penelope knew he really wanted to laugh. "Chief Purcell and Ms. Hammer *did* have a rather loud discussion in the hallway." He ignored Jake's snort of amusement. "But mostly it was because we got the toxicology back."

"No alcohol," Penelope hazarded.

"Correct."

"And...?" There had to be something else that helped exonerate Edward. They'd already known about the alcohol.

"Pain pills. Not enough to kill him, but definitely more than he would have taken on his own."

"Which explains why he didn't call for help when he started feeling sick." It was nice to have one piece of the puzzle in place, but that still didn't give the police a reason to release Edward. "Wait. Pills?" Edward had mentioned Harold had been upset about pills, but she still found it hard to believe.

"The pharmacist confirmed it was his prescription when

we checked. She thought it was odd, too, but he definitely picked them up."

Brutus nudged Jake, who responded by switching the scent cue and another treat behind his back, and then holding out his closed fists. Brutus snuffled at the hand holding the baggie and Jake gave him the treat.

Penelope was still stuck on what Brian had said. "But that doesn't clear Edward. Harold was already accusing him of stealing his pills."

"No, but the timing does. Two different neighbors saw Edward leave that day. Half the street had heard them fighting, so that's not a surprise. The pathologist says Harold couldn't have taken, or been given, the pills until at least four hours later. Edward still could have come back later, so he's not in the clear yet, but it makes his visit for lunch less important." He was silent for a moment. "Plus he has a really good lawyer, and Purcell is worried about the department getting sued less than a week after Jake left."

"Did *you* know that Edward's girlfriend Tweetie was Rebecca Wallingstone's daughter?"

Jake's head shot up. "Rebecca Wallingstone?" Brutus had to bump the hand with the lemon scent twice before Jake noticed and gave the dog his treat. "I used to love her movies."

"This does not shock me."

Brian shook his head. "I'd never heard of her before."

Jake was hiding a grin, only partially successfully. "She was a great actress."

"What he means is that she was famous for taking roles that required full nudity, in the time before the internet," Penelope translated. "Though some of her movies were actually pretty good."

Brutus took Jake's inattention as a sign that the training session was over. He flopped down on top of Brian's feet, nearly knocking Brian over in the process. Jake didn't notice. "We should have a movie night."

"Just pick a night when I'm booked on an overnight pet sitting job so I don't have to listen to you complain about how old it made you feel. So someone fed Harold pain pills and botulism toxin and either waited for him to fall asleep or came back later to throw around some vodka. That seems like a lot of extra risk. Especially since they had to have known the coroner could easily measure the alcohol in the blood."

"The pathologist, not the coroner, but yes." Brian worked one foot out from underneath the dog and moved it backward to brace himself. "On the other hand, if we had gotten sloppy, it might have worked. And we might not have preserved the scene enough to find the inconsistencies if we hadn't been lucky." He reached down to scratch Brutus's belly and roll the dog forward enough to free his other foot. "I need to get back to work. Rebecca Wallingstone, you said her name was?"

"Yes. I think she and her husband run a winery these days."

Penelope and Jake watched Brian get back in his car and drive away while Brutus rolled in the grass.

Jake frowned. "Did I hear you say she named her daughter Tweetie?"

CHAPTER 14

*B*y the time she paused for a late lunch the next day, Penelope had jogged three miles with Heidi, scooped seven litter boxes, medicated two dogs and a cat, and taken another three dogs for more sedate strolls around their neighborhoods, all so she could free up a block of time in the afternoon to go to the soap-making class. By scheduling the class on a weekday afternoon, Skye was probably limiting her customers to stay at home parents and retirees, but Penelope thought that was probably the right audience anyhow.

The food left over from the retirement party was starting to lose its appeal, both because she'd been eating it every day and because everything had achieved an equal level of sogginess. She was toasting bread for a sandwich when Jake and Brutus came in. The dog barreled to his water dish, and Jake sat down at the table with the leash and tackle box in front of him.

"How did class go?" She'd warned Jake that morning not to expect Brutus to be at his most focused — Brutus had more-or-less mastered the first scent cue exercise at home, but in a public place he might well act like it was a new thing he'd never seen before. "Do you want a sandwich?"

"I'll grab something in a minute. The good news is that Brutus wasn't able to get into this." He patted the tackle box. "So we don't need to go into debt buying more vials of essential oils just yet."

"I notice that leaves a fair amount of room for the bad news." Penelope spread peanut butter on one piece of bread, and then added sour pickle and jalapeño slices before topping it with a layer of potato chips. She added the top piece of bread and cut it in half diagonally before placing it on a plate with a handful of baby carrots.

Jake eyed her sandwich. "If I tried to eat that I'd end up in the emergency room."

"And yet Brutus could eat it with a dead gopher chaser and be absolutely fine. Comparison is the thief of joy."

Jake snorted and took a carrot. "Your dog didn't completely forget what he was doing in class. He wasn't the best, but he might have come in second."

"You realize it's not supposed to be a competition, right?"

"That's the attitude that losers have." Jake smiled and took another carrot. "There's a pug in class."

Penelope blinked, trying to imagine someone using a pug as a working dog. "You're *not* going to tell me that our dog was beaten by a pug."

"Remember, it's not a competition. Comparison is the thief of joy."

"Right, but still. A pug?"

"As it happens, no. The best dog was a beagle. The pug owner had one of those retractable leashes that you love so much."

Penelope cringed. Nothing good ever came from retractable leashes.

"And of course the pug's owner wasn't paying attention

most of the time, and her dog was running around humping the other dogs. Or their legs, anyhow. The pug is pretty short."

"Brutus didn't hurt him, did he?" Brutus was a pretty easygoing mastiff, but every once in a while he took a dislike to another dog. He was always good about escalating slowly, but some dogs didn't notice social cues. And a pug, already prone to breathing and spinal problems just due to bad breeding, might be injured even if Brutus wasn't trying.

"No. Your dog stepped on the leash and then peed on him. Just absolutely hosed him down." Jake smiled as he thought about it. "Luckily the pug's face was out of the direct stream or he might have drowned."

"How'd that go over with the owner?"

"Not great." Jake shrugged. "But our instructor had already asked her twice to keep the leash locked at five feet, so I think I won the moral victory."

Penelope watched him as she ate another bite of her sandwich. "So you had the moral high ground, your dog didn't otherwise disgrace himself, and you don't have to buy any more supplies. Why are you acting so mopey?"

"I'm fine. I'm just feeling a little old."

Assuming his malaise was related to retiring, Penelope was about to reassure him that he could have a whole new career ahead of him when a suspicion popped into her head. "You watched one of those Rebecca Wallingstone movies, didn't you?"

"I was feeling nostalgic." He let out a profound sigh. "Maybe it's because I've spent so many years responding to disasters. You know that one scene where she's in the rain?"

"Of course." Movie memorabilia companies *still* made money off that poster.

"She used to look sexy. Now all I thought was that she looked malnourished and miserable, and just entirely too young to be running around out there, especially with her co-star. He had to be at least twenty years older."

"Thirty-four, in fact."

Jake sighed again. He pushed himself to his feet and went to the refrigerator. "At least you'll never feel like this watching him in a movie. You'd have to be over one hundred before the 'half your age plus seven' rule excludes him."

"I don't think that helps your case as much as you think it does."

Jake pulled out the container of pastries. "I think these might be ready for the garbage disposal." He shoved it back in the refrigerator and closed the door. "That guy was *my* age when they made that film?"

"Yes. But you're sexier."

"At least I'm not running around chasing teenagers." He slathered a layer of peanut butter on a piece of bread, put an orderly row of banana slices on top, added another piece of bread, and then carefully cut off the crusts. "Thank you for holding off on saying 'I told you so'."

"I wasn't even thinking it." When Jake held her gaze she cracked. "Okay, maybe just a little bit. But I was thinking about other stuff, so I might have completely forgotten to say it anyway."

"What could possibly be more important than an 'I told you so'?" He seemed back to his normal equanimity. "This is about Harold Stone, isn't it?"

"I was trying to figure out why someone would bother coming back a second time. Because it would be a huge risk. If you drug and poison someone and leave before they start to feel the effects, nobody would be able to prove anything. But if someone saw you leaving after the person was almost certainly showing symptoms, there's no question of who did it. So why come back?"

"Assuming it wasn't just to try to make it look like he had

been drinking too heavily to get help..." Jake nodded when she opened her mouth to protest. "I agree with you there. It feels like something they did because they were already there. So if we ignore that, the two main reasons I can come up with are because they needed to go back to make sure Harold hadn't left a note, or they needed to get something that they couldn't get while they were there the first time."

Penelope regarded him suspiciously. "Why are you being so helpful? I thought you would give me your standard 'leave it to the police' line."

"Because I know Brian's already looking into it. You won't be making yourself a target by snooping because the detectives have already done their own snooping."

"Good. Then as an intellectual exercise, you can help me come up with reasons someone might go back. The obvious one is money."

"Agreed. But unlikely in this case because there was three thousand dollars in cash in the fire safe. His ex-wife —"

"Amelia." She smiled at him. "You can consider the lecture about not defining women by their relationships to men as given."

"Thank you. Amelia said that was about the amount of cash he normally kept at home for emergencies."

"Huh. I always figured Harold would be one of those people who kept his savings in gold bars because he was convinced the banks were about to collapse." When Jake raised an eyebrow she shook her head. "Nah, probably not. I've never known one of the gold standard people who didn't lecture everyone else about it, and that wasn't one of Harold's speeches." She thought about it for a minute. "It could still be someone who was after the money but didn't know about the fire safe or couldn't get into it. But this seems like a lot of planning to do for three thousand dollars."

"Agreed."

"Maybe there was something else in the safe?"

"Years ago, he also kept his journals there, but Amelia said that stopped when the kids left home. As far as anyone knows, it was just the cash and things like his birth certificate and passport, and that's all there."

"And there wasn't anything valuable missing in the rest of the house, I assume, or Brian would have mentioned it."

"It doesn't sound like there was anything particularly valuable in the house to begin with. A lot of things that someone might take to sell for a few bucks here or there, but it didn't look like any of those things were missing."

"That's more of a spur of the moment cash grab anyhow. Whoever did this is a planner."

Jake leaned over to look at the oven clock. "Speaking of planning, didn't you have to be somewhere soon?"

"Thank you." Penelope checked her phone and jumped to her feet. "I'm off to learn how to make soap. There might still be room in the class if you want to join."

"I thought maybe I'd take a nap instead."

"Suit yourself. Don't let your garbage disposal eat all the leftovers at one time." She grinned at his guilty start, grabbed the tote bag of supplies, and ran out the door.

CHAPTER 15

For something that had been added to the schedule at the last minute, Skye's cold press soap making class was more full than Penelope had expected. She was one of the last to arrive. With memories of attending craft demonstrations for mothers of toddlers just trying to keep sane, Penelope was surprised at how dressed up the other members of the class were. If these women — and they were all women — were here merely because they were in desperate need of adult conversation, they were doing a better job hiding it than Penelope ever had. She recognized a few faces from the rose garden committee auction that Esther had dragged her to. They didn't have children, or even grandchildren, at home. They just had the money and time to take an expensive class in the middle of the day.

Penelope thought about living like that and decided she would be bored within two days. Pet sitting and delivering mail might not be glamorous jobs, but they kept her too busy to worry about little things, like if her soap-making supplies were good enough.

She followed two women through the shop and out the

open back door to the fenced-in patio, where tables had been set up. Skye walked out from the shop behind her, and stood in front of a smaller table that overlooked the others. Every face on the patio turned to look at her. "I think we're all here now. Penelope, there's a seat open next to Moira. Here you go." She held out a wooden tub that had been one of the supplies provided in the materials fee.

Penelope took the last spot available and unloaded everything from her public radio fundraiser tote bag: stick blender, bowl, bath towel, spatula, whisk, rubber gloves, and safety goggles.

The largest item was the hideous yellow-green Pyrex mixing bowl from the 1970s, gifted to Jake by his aunt who had a habit of wrapping random household goods and presenting them to him on holidays and birthdays. The bath towel was ragged and yellow with bleach stains, one of the ones they used to clean up Brutus. The rubber spatula had a clear set of bite marks marring the handle, a reminder of a puppy that Penelope had been taking care of for a few weeks, and the whisk had clearly been bent and straightened, a mystery which neither Penelope nor Jake could explain. The stick blender looked out of place in its newness; it had been a wedding present, and since neither one had made soup yet, the cord was still held in a neat bundle with the original twist tie.

Everyone else had either clear glass bowls, or pristine plastic containers with color-coded lids, and towels that looked like they had been pulled from the guest bathroom before they had ever been used. Penelope didn't envy these women their free time, but she did covet the plastic containers. Just once she wanted to be able to put leftovers away without digging through the container drawer for a lid that would fit.

"I'm surprised you'd bring that here," the woman beside

her said as she looked at the Pyrex bowl. Penelope had seen her at the dog park with two Cavalier King Charles spaniels, where she would walk around the perimeter twice, the dogs following two steps behind, and then load them back into her Subaru hatchback and drive off. "I'd be afraid I'd accidentally knock it off the edge of the table and have to find a new one."

Penelope waited for a laugh that didn't come. Apparently the woman was serious. "If things can't be used for their intended purpose, what's the point of having them?" She tried to keep her tone light so it didn't sound like criticism.

The other woman smiled. "Good point. May I?" She gestured to the bowl and Penelope nodded.

"I guess I should confess that my husband and I have been sort of hoping that someday it would break so we'd feel justified in throwing it out. It was a gift from his aunt, but it's also incredibly ugly."

Moira had picked up the bowl to examine it, but now she held it at arms length and cocked her head. "It is, isn't it? But it's worth quite a lot if you ever want to sell it." She placed it carefully on the table again.

"Skye called you Moira? I'm Penelope."

"Nice to meet you."

At the front of the class, Skye had donned her safety goggles and rubber gloves, somehow still managing to look glamorous. "Welcome, everyone. Today we're going to make a soap with a coconut oil base, which you'll find is really nice on your skin. You can pick your dye, scent, and botanicals in just a moment, but first I want to go through the process of mixing the lye, so you can do this safely at home."

Penelope perked up. She hadn't realized soap-making involved dangerous chemicals. Her only previous exposure to lye had been in the pages of mystery and thriller novels, where it was used to dispose of inconvenient bodies. She'd always assumed the acquisition was one of those difficult details that the author had just hand-waved away — she hadn't realized you could just go out and buy it.

"I've already measured out the amount I want into this tub." Sky tapped the lid of a plastic container that Penelope was pretty sure wasn't recyclable. "Now I'm going to measure out the water..." She paused and poured water into a plastic container that had a matching lid next to it. "I have my safety equipment on. The most important thing is what?"

In almost perfect unison, the rest of the class intoned "Always add the sodium hydroxide to the water."

Penelope glanced around, somewhat unnerved. It felt more like a chant than a hobby instruction.

"Correct. The most important thing is that you always want to add the sodium hydroxide to the water, never the other way around." She pulled the lid off the smaller tub and dumped the granules into the liquid, stirring with a whisk. "If you do it the wrong way around, it can splatter all over and if this gets on your skin you can be badly burned. So always have the water in the bowl first, and then add the sodium hydroxide."

Penelope looked around again. Everyone other than Moira watched closely as Skye stirred the contents of her bowl. From the intensity of their stares, Penelope expected something exciting to happen, but as far as she could tell, they were just watching someone stir a container of liquid with a whisk.

Skye finished dissolving the granules, put the whisk in a waiting bowl, and put the lid on the container. "As you know, this reaction causes a fair bit of heat, and since we don't want to wait around for it to cool down today, I've premixed the correct amount of lye for our recipe for everyone here. I'll distribute those while you go pick out your dye, scent, and botanical. All the choices are on the table next to the door.

After everyone is back at their tables, I'll go through the next steps."

As the people nearest the door jumped up and crowded around the supplies, it occurred to Penelope there was a reason the last available seat had been at the other edge of the group. Penelope followed Moira to the end of the line. "Why do I have a feeling that we're not going to have much to choose from?"

Moira touched the side of her nose. "There's usually only one or two of the more expensive things. It's not so bad, though, as long as you don't mind lavender."

"It seems like everyone here already knows what they're doing." Penelope had thought the idea of the class was to teach people how to make soap on their own. Surely it couldn't take multiple sessions.

"Oh, this is the fifth..." Moira paused. "No, sixth soap making class that Skye has offered. She uses a recipe with different oils each time, so it varies a bit. Mostly it's just a chance to get out of the house for a while."

"But what is everyone doing with all the soap?"

Humor flashed in Moira's eyes. "*I* have a garage full of bars that are curing. I suspect some of the others toss it straight into the garbage when they get home, just like the sourdough classes, and the egg painting class. The waste used to drive Harold mad. Not to speak ill of the dead or anything, but this store will be a lot calmer without him. I'm pretty sure Skye switched to soap making because all the scents used to drive him out of the store. I heard him complaining to a customer about perfumes in cleaning products, and the next thing you know, we're making scented soap."

By the time they made it to the front of the line, all that was left were dried lavender flowers, and lavender scent. Penelope tried to decide if she wanted to go with a more traditional purple, or head off-piste with yellow or even green. She finally grabbed purple and headed back to her seat where there were now tubs labeled "lye" and "coconut oil" next to her things.

Skye straightened her posture and the patio quieted. "Before we start mixing, if you aren't using a silicone mold, make sure you have lined your form."

Nearly everyone else in the class had brought flexible silicone molds that would create individual bars shaped like various creatures. Penelope wondered what Harold had said when he'd seen those. Somehow she didn't think he had been a fan of silicone molds. The only other person still using the wooden loaf-like form that came as part of the class supplies was Moira, who pulled a roll of brown freezer paper from her bag and handed it to her. "Use whatever you need."

"Thanks." Penelope tore off a strip and folded it until it fit inside the wooden mold.

Meanwhile Skye was pouring items into her bowl. "Remember, you only want to blend it briefly. If you blend it too long, it will start to set before you can get it in the mold, and you won't be able to swirl it or do any other flourishes." She immersed the stick blender and pulsed it. "Make sure you don't incorporate any air."

Penelope looked around to see how other people were managing that, but the entire group was holding still and watching Skye. Even though it was a group of adults, Penelope was impressed. She'd had to teach crafts to her son's scout troop, and keeping everyone's attention was not an easy thing. From what Moira had said, most of these women had heard these instructions before.

"Once you start seeing trace, carefully pour it into your molds, and then you can do any artwork or add botanicals or crystals on the top." She knocked the stick blender against the side of the bowl and set it down, then poured the mixture into a silicone form.

"Once you start seeing what?" Penelope whispered.

Moira kept her voice low. "Trace. It's the point when you can still see it if you drizzle it on top of the rest."

Skye had finished scraping the last bit with her silicone spatula, and she drew off her gloves and goggles. "I need to go help some customers, but I'll be back in a few minutes if anyone has any questions." She disappeared back into the store, and the noise level instantly rose, as if a spell had been broken.

Penelope pulled on the safety goggles Jake used for woodworking projects. Everything was immediately blurry, but she could still see well enough to work. Over the noise of talking and the whir of stick blenders pulsing, she said, "Skye has quite a presence."

"She does, doesn't she? She's the only person I ever saw shut her father down when he was ranting to someone." Moira had poured all her supplies into the bowl and pulsed the blender a few times. She raised it above the surface and let the thin purple liquid drip down. "See how it vanishes immediately. There's no trace yet." She blended a few more seconds, then repeated the process. This time the line of liquid was visible briefly before submerging. "Now it has trace."

"Got it, thanks." Penelope pulled on the gloves and dumped everything other than the lavender into the bowl. Only after she'd added it did she realize that the dye wasn't purple, but orange. She shrugged. Even when she tried to be conventional, her fingers betrayed her. She put the stick blender in and turned it on. Tiny air bubbles radiated from the center of the mixture. "Oops."

Moira looked over. "Next time you do this, if you swish it around before you turn it on, that gets the air out." She went back to swirling designs on the top of her soap with the back end of a tiny paint brush.

Penelope tried that, and pulsed the blender a bit more. The mixture lightened as the reaction progressed. The bubbles she'd added didn't disappear. The whole thing looked a bit like an orange creamsicle, but when she drizzled some over the top, the mixture acted like icing and stayed visible.

She glanced around. Some people were sprinkling their botanicals on the top. If she did that, half of it would fall off later. She dumped the bag into the bowl and used the unpowered stick blender to stir it all together.

The mixture was already stiffening when she dumped it into the mold, and instead of pouring in an even stream like all the ones around her, Penelope had to level out the part already in the mold in order to make space for the rest of it. Moira helped hold the bowl so she could get the last of it in.

They both looked at the result, a bubbly orange mess with dark lumps where the dried lavender showed through. Penelope stripped off her gloves and goggles. "There we go. Another skill mastered."

Moira bit her lip. Then she covered her mouth while she laughed. "I'm sorry. I'm sure it will be better when it cures."

Penelope squinted at the mixture. "I'm fairly certain this is as good as it's going to get. That's okay. If I just wanted nice-looking soap I would have bought some from the shop. This has... character."

That set off another round of laughter in Moira. She dabbed at her eyes as she tried to compose herself. "You're one of those people who knows how to have fun. So what are you doing *here?*"

"I was curious." She didn't add that she was curious about Skye, not making soap. "Why are *you* here? You don't seem to enjoy it." After she'd played the words back to herself, Penelope realized that sentence had been less than tactful, but Moira didn't seem to notice.

"When my wife was ill, I promised her I wouldn't sit around the house all day after she died. She was the outgoing one, you know, always dragging me along on hikes with our friends and parties and those sorts of things." Moira looked around the patio at the other women. "I come here because it's *easy*. They all know each other and have common interests. I'm sure they would include me if I made any effort at all, but when I don't, they just ignore me. It's peaceful." She laughed a little and looked at Penelope. "That probably makes no sense to you."

"Actually, it makes a lot of sense."

"Someday I may go back to work just to have something to do, but it's not a financial necessity, and it's hard to hold down a job when you may need to lie down and stare at the ceiling for three hours at any moment." Moira gave a small self-deprecating laugh. "So I make soap. And pine needle baskets. And spin yarn. And make paper." She cocked her head. "I'm forgetting a few."

"What kind of work do you do?"

"I was a forensic accountant." Moira smiled when she caught Penelope's glance back at the store. "Ah, that kind of curious."

Penelope winced. She'd been hoping nobody would notice her interest in anything other than soap. Too many of the women in the class seemed to look up to Skye. Then she looked at the lumpy orange monstrosity she had created and realized that people would have difficulty believing she had any interest *in* soap.

"It wouldn't surprise me if there were some shenanigans in the accounts." Moira covered the top of her soap tray with a piece of cardboard, and wrapped the whole thing in a towel. "You want to keep your soap insulated for the next day or so. Otherwise you get different layers showing up as it cures."

They both looked at Penelope's offering. Penelope wound the dog-bathing towel around it, mostly to hide it from everyone else in the class. She was starting to feel strangely protective of this ugly thing.

Skye came back out. "How is everyone doing? If you need to cut your soap into smaller pieces, do that tomorrow. That will give it enough time to cure, but it will still be soft enough to cut with a kitchen knife. Any questions?" She waited, but nobody offered any. "It's been lovely to see you all. Remember, the new classes are opening up Friday morning bright and early, and they're going to fill up quickly. Next month I'll be adding in classes on weaving, and I know some of you will be excited about that. In the meantime, I just got a new shipment of silicone forms, if anyone is interested." Most of the class followed her back into the shop.

"She's wasted here." Moira started putting her bowl and implements back in her bag. "She should be running a cult. Or just a pyramid scheme. Though she's probably cleaning up even here." Penelope must have looked dubious. "She passes all the costs of the classes on to her students, plus a hefty fee on top of that. Plus the monthly subscription that most of them are paying. And then all of the extras like the soap forms. By switching to a new craft every month or two, she's getting a regular bump in income. Trust me, if this shop had been breaking even by selling granola mix and showing people how to can their vegetables before, it's making a small fortune now."

That was interesting, but not evidence of anything nefarious. Penelope thought she probably ought to be congratulating Skye on being such a successful entrepreneur. "She certainly does better than I do. Walking dogs," she added when Moira raised an eyebrow in query. Penelope dug out one of her business cards and gave it to her. "Maybe I should start selling gourmet biscuits on the side, or something."

Moira tucked the card in her purse. "You get to spend most of your time with dogs and cats, though. It might be worth it as long as you can still pay the bills." She nodded at Penelope's bag of supplies. "Let everything sit for a day and finish turning into soap, and then it will all rinse right off."

They made their way back through the shop, maneuvering around all the other people waiting to pay for new silicone forms of baby raccoons, giant daisies, and — she squinted — yes, that was an entire tray of phallic objects. Skye definitely knew what would sell to her audience.

Penelope took a moment to look at the entire store. Would it really take Skye all night to rearrange the stock? According to the security video, it had. That seemed a little excessive, but maybe Skye had also been wiping down walls or doing one of the other hundreds of things maintaining a store required.

Outside, Moira opened the trunk of a BMW and loaded her things. "See you at the dog park?"

"Call me if you want to meet up. I'm usually there at least once during the day." Penelope lifted her bag. "Thanks for all your help today."

"I'm sorry it turned out like... that." Moira started giggling again.

Penelope laughed and headed for home.

CHAPTER 16

*T*wenty-four hours of curing did not improve the soap.

Penelope turned it onto the cutting board and peeled the freezer paper from the sides. It still looked like a lumpy creamsicle on the top, but having the whole thing exposed made it also vaguely reminiscent of flesh. The whole room smelled of lavender.

"Ah." Jake rubbed his lower lip with his hand. "That was an interesting color choice."

"I thought I had grabbed purple." Penelope leaned over to open the kitchen window. Presumably the scent would fade as the soap cured, but for now it was too powerful for an enclosed space. "Now I have to cut it into bars and then the bars will cure for another few months. I think." The knife went through the soap with a little pressure, but the cut edges took some effort to get apart.

They looked at the slice.

The lavender buds mixed into the soap had turned nearly black. Also, it looked like the towel hadn't insulated enough, because there was a color gradation, with the center looking almost pink and uneven layers showing the progression to the outer orange.

"Are those... rat turds?" Jake was still hiding his mouth with his hand, but his voice was impressively even.

Penelope cleared her throat. "I can see why you might think that. Those are lavender buds. They looked different yesterday." In their current form they really *did* look like rat droppings. She forced the knife through the next slice and pried it away from the rest of the mass. "This is a coconut oil-based soap. It's good for your skin."

Jake's voice was fervent. "If you think I'm putting that anywhere near my unprotected flesh, we need to have a talk."

"I was sort of hoping it might turn out to be one of those 'It's so ugly that it's cute' things." The last words came out more forcefully as she cut off another bar. "Maybe it will get better as it cures." She finished cutting and placed all the bars on a piece of cardboard. "Can you put this up in the rafters in the garage? I don't want your dog to eat them."

"Out of morbid curiosity, are you more worried about the soap or the dog in that scenario?" Jake picked up the cardboard but didn't leave. "Does it have to be the garage? Everything is going to smell like flowers."

"Probably only for a week or so. I think it will calm down after that." Penelope had no idea if that was true. "If you don't feel like climbing up there, I can do it." She reached up to take the cardboard from him.

He lifted it out of her reach. "I'll do it."

Penelope smiled at him. They both knew the stacking of everything in the garage rafters was his domain, and he'd have to be incapacitated before he would let anybody else do it. "Treat those gently. This is probably the most expensive soap you're ever going to see."

He regarded the soap, and without one hand to hide his face, she could see when his mouth twitched. "I'm not convinced that teaching is Skye's forte. Have you considered suggesting that she find a different line of work?"

"Points to you for suggesting that the problem was with the teacher and not the student." Penelope followed him out to the garage where the odor of dust and laundry detergent battled against the lavender. "But by my calculations, Skye is making a killing on these classes." She told him about the subscription fees and additional equipment expenses as he climbed the ladder built into the wall and began shifting things around.

"You realize if Skye's making money at the shop, it makes it less likely for her to have money as a motive, right?" The sound of a cardboard flap being opened followed. "Why are we saving a box of plastic robots?"

"They're Seth's. I keep forgetting to give them to him when he's here."

"Does he *want* them?"

"I have no idea. He's probably forgotten about them completely, but if I just get rid of them, it will turn out that they're all collector's items." She heard Jake close the box again. "Speaking of collector's items, did you know the ugly bowl is worth something?"

Jake's head appeared. "The yellow one? Really?"

"It's more green than yellow, but yes, that bowl. Moira said they were expensive to replace."

"Who would buy that?" His voice got quieter. "Maybe we can sell this soap to the same people."

"Sorry, honey, did you say something?"

"No, just thinking out loud about the best way to arrange things." He started back down the ladder. "Do I know Moira?"

"Probably not. I met her at class, but I've seen her at the dog park." She waited until he was back on the ground and then reached over to detach a cobweb from his hair. "We could probably get a deal on prettier soap from her."

Jake enfolded her in a hug. "Penelope, we could get a deal on prettier soap from the supermarket." He kissed her temple. "In bulk."

"True." The smell of lavender was starting to win the war. She pulled out her phone to check the time. "I have to go walk some dogs."

"You're just trying to leave before I notice the smell."

Penelope grinned, stood on her toes, and gave him a quick kiss. "Maybe today would be a good day to open the door and sweep all the dust out."

"Or just open the door and sit on a lawn chair and drink beer."

Penelope put the chance of Jake spending the afternoon sitting around at almost zero. "Just keep the beer away from your dog."

CHAPTER 17

*T*he next morning Penelope had been sitting on the rectory floor with Spot for half an hour when she heard familiar steps coming up to the door. "It's open," she called.

Jake pushed the door open with one hand and held up a covered platter in the other. "I wasn't sure if you were coming back home first, so I brought you the sausage rolls." He put the platter down on the table. "And maybe CJ wants some. The recipe made more than I thought it would."

Penelope slipped out from under the dog and stood up. "Congratulations, you managed to relax in your retirement an entire day longer than I thought you would." She caught a slight tensing of his shoulders. "Or maybe not. What did I miss?"

"I might have set up a new system for your business on the computer yesterday." He held up his hands, palms out. "You don't have to use it, if you don't want to. It was more of a proof of concept, to see if I could integrate your calendar with the spreadsheet and the banking software."

Penelope looked up at him. "You did all that *yesterday?*"

"You're not mad."

Penelope waved that thought away and picked up one of the sausage rolls. "You know how much I hate working that stuff out at the end of the month." She took a bite, paused, and chewed slowly. Egg, cheese, dough, but mostly... "What kind of sausage is this?" She was fairly certain she already knew the answer.

"Boar. Brian gave me some a while ago. I thought I'd better use it before it went bad."

Brian had spent a weekend hunting wild boar with some friends as part of dealing with the implosion of his marriage. Disguised as civic duty since the wild pig population had become a danger to hikers, the weekend had been a success in that Brian had decided that it was time to quit hanging out with the college friends who had never grown up. But he *had* managed to kill a boar and had gifted the meat to all of his friends when he returned. The sausage had been in the back of the freezer only because Penelope hadn't had the courage to throw it out. The meat overpowered every dish she'd ever tried it in. She narrowed her eyes when she saw Jake casually looking around the room. "You were hoping for donuts."

"CJ doesn't even like them."

"I'm sure he'd be happy enough to give you some if you just asked. You don't need to assault him with these first."

Spot scrambled to her feet and ran to the door. Sure enough, CJ opened the door a few seconds later, though Penelope hadn't heard anyone coming.

"Jake! How are you doing this morning?" He automatically caressed Spot's head as he walked in. "Would you like a cup of coffee? And you brought breakfast!"

"That's up for debate." Penelope poured coffee for them both. "He used the boar sausage that's been aging in our freezer because it ruins everything it touches."

"And yet it's still somehow less scary than that soap I put up in the rafters yesterday," Jake said.

Penelope laughed and almost choked on her coffee. "I took a soap making class at Homespun Harold's a couple of days ago," she explained to CJ, who was eating one of the sausage rolls with evident enjoyment. "The results were... mixed."

"That's right. You found Harold's body, didn't you?" CJ took a second roll. "So you wanted to learn about his daughter."

"Can't I just have wanted to learn to make soap?" She tried to keep a straight face as both men looked skeptical. "Fine, I wanted to learn more about Skye. Mostly I just learned that she's far better at running a business than I ever have been."

CJ looked off into the air. "I don't think I've ever met Skye. Amelia and her new husband come to services every so often, and I'll be performing the marriage ceremony for Edward and Tweetie next summer." His face lit up. "It's going to be at her family's winery. It sounds quite lovely. It would be nice to be able to live in a place like that." He looked fondly at the kitchen, with its worn and antiquated furnishings. "Though I can't complain. And it would be hard to gather enough people for a congregation in such a remote place."

"You know Tweetie's mother is Rebecca Wallingstone, right?"

"That's what Esther told me, but I have to admit, I don't see enough movies to know who that is. I guess I should probably watch one before the wedding, just to be polite."

Jake cleared his throat. "I think they might just be a product of their time. I wouldn't bother."

"Jake's just mad because he tried to watch one this week and ended up feeling like an old man."

"Ah, that's why Esther didn't press me to watch them." He took another roll. "Tweetie is a lovely child. Very kind. I think she and Edward will be quite happy together, and he deserves some happiness. It can't have been easy growing up in that household."

Penelope opened the pantry and took out a large pink box with grease stains coming through. Jake deserved a donut or two for finding someone who liked boar sausage. "You knew Harold then?"

"A difficult man. Of course he wasn't a member of the church, but we met a few times." His mouth tightened. "He once accused me of poisoning people because I included processed food and some candy bars in the food baskets. As if hungry people were supposed to somehow afford organic food and then have the time and energy to make things from scratch." He shook his head. "Half of the people getting those baskets don't have anything other than a microwave."

Penelope held out the open box to Jake. "See? Natural food and recycling. It was always one or the other."

"Oh yes, we had a few run-ins about recycling as well." CJ sighed. "I know the breakdown of a marriage is never a cause for celebration, but I can't help thinking that it would have been better for the children if she'd left him earlier."

Penelope had known plenty of divorces that had been a cause for celebration, including the one that ended her own first marriage, but she supposed they would have to disagree about that. "For some reason I'd always assumed that he left her." She thought back to the scene outside Harold's house, when Amelia seemed to be going through the motions of comforting Skye just because she was supposed to. "She's always seemed like one of those people that just puts up with everything."

CJ rocked a hand back and forth. "It was when they were looking to license some of the brands. Harold was traveling more, and one of the buyer's representatives was an attractive young woman. I'm not sure anything ever happened, but he was besotted and Amelia finally left him. And then of course, after the company paperwork had all been signed, the representative disappeared and Harold tried to get Amelia back, but it was too late."

"Amelia should send a gift basket to that woman every year for the rest of her life. She never would have escaped, otherwise."

"Possibly. Though maybe she would have started standing up for herself eventually. Edward was worried about having both parents at the wedding because there had been some recent tension about the business. I think it was the first time I'd ever heard of Amelia arguing with anyone."

Jake looked up from his perusal of donuts, suddenly interested.

"Oh, not enough to kill anyone over. But when they divorced, she had ended up with 49 percent of the business, which meant she had a fairly even split of the profits, but Harold could override any decisions he wanted to. And it sounded like he'd been making some questionable choices lately."

Penelope raised an eyebrow. "Another young representative taking him for a ride?"

"That, I don't know. I certainly never saw him with anyone, but I don't think I've seen him more than once or twice in the last year since I stopped taking Spotty to the p-a-r-k." The Dalmatian lifted her head, clearly having heard this workaround many times before. "The arthritis makes her grumpy when the younger dogs jump on her," CJ explained to Jake, "so we had to stop going."

Penelope pressed on, not wanting to get sidetracked into talk of the dog park at the moment. "I wish I knew how much money was involved. If Homespun Harold's is more or less breaking even, there's not much financial motive. But if Harold was just bad at paying his bills and he was really worth millions, that's different."

"Not really." Jake pushed the donut box to the other side of the table. "Most homicides for financial gain are for amounts that are less than what a decent defense lawyer would charge in an hour or two. CJ is just as likely to be murdered for the spare cash in the cookie jar as someone with millions is."

"Ah, but it's in the flour canister, not the cookie jar, so I should be safe enough."

"And you wouldn't try to stop someone who broke in to steal it," Penelope added. The Episcopal church was never going to be flush with money, but CJ only repaired or replaced what was absolutely necessary because he felt there were better uses for that money out in his congregation. Penelope knew there was one committee that was secretly raising money to renovate the kitchen — secretly, because the last time they had raised money for the project, CJ had diverted it to the rent relief program.

"Well, no. If someone is forced to resort to stealing cash from a church, they probably need it far more than I do."

Penelope thought about Jake's words for a moment. "So you're saying that I don't need to know anything about Harold's finances to figure out motive."

Jake sighed and took another donut. "No. I'm saying leave it to the police. But statistically, it's probably a close friend or a family member. Since it sounds like Harold didn't have any friends, it's almost certainly a family member. If I was blindly betting without any facts, I'd put my money on the ex-wife. Who could hate you more than your spouse?" He winked at Penelope.

Penelope smiled at him. "Who, indeed?"

CJ looked troubled. "But Amelia would never…"

She shrugged. "Maybe not, but what's the saying — still waters run deep? She and Harold ran those canning classes together for years, so she would definitely know how to produce botulism. And if she had finally gotten to the point of pushing back against him... Amelia's probably got about thirty years of rage bottled up inside her. I mean, *I* would have killed Harold within a week if I'd been married to him."

Both men looked vaguely alarmed.

"Oh, relax. I'm not exactly still waters." She paused. "Though, honestly, I think if Amelia had snapped there would be a lot more blood at the scene. I think CJ's right. Amelia probably didn't do it."

"An alibi would be a more meaningful defense." Jake paused. "Hypothetically, of course. Because I'm leaving this to the police."

"Brian didn't sound too thrilled with anyone's alibi. To be fair, who has a good alibi at night? Either you're alone, or you're with someone who hopefully likes you enough to lie for you." She fluttered her lashes at Jake. "I'd give you an alibi for any night."

"Honey, if I ever have to depend on you for an alibi, I might as well just turn myself in and confess. There's a non-zero chance that the detective would call you Mrs. Wheeler and you would be so busy lecturing them about women having names in their own right that you would never get around to telling them I was with you." He paused. "Do you need help rinsing something out of your eye?"

Penelope drew in a breath to argue, then blew it back out. "You're probably right. You should make sure you don't do anything that requires me to alibi you. And of course, I never do anything wrong, so I would never need you to alibi me."

Jake blinked and wisely stayed silent.

Penelope stood up. "The east side mail carrier is taking the day off to recover from some big party her kids were throwing, so I have to go check on a few pets and then deliver some very important junk mail. Spot, you be a good girl. CJ, I'll see you tomorrow morning. And Jake, I'll see you at lunch if you're there. Don't feed Brutus all the boar meat just to get rid of it."

She waited a moment to see if he would look guilty, but he merely smiled.

CHAPTER 18

*P*enelope had delivered all the boxes for her route, and had settled into the steady rhythm that made the rest of the deliveries go by quickly; there was just enough time between each house to get the next set of mail out of her bag and glance through it to see if there was anything interesting before arriving at the mailbox and then starting the cycle over again.

College brochures had been coming to the Cortez house for a while — mostly state universities, but a few colleges farther away that were probably aspirational given the modest house and four younger siblings. John was on the junior varsity football team, so a sports scholarship probably wasn't in his future, but academic superstars weren't promoted as heavily in the local media. Without having any children in the school system any more, Penelope didn't keep up on who was at the top of their class. Esther would probably know.

Most of the out-of-state brochures featured schools near popular beaches. Penelope couldn't fault him on that choice. She'd chosen her college because her high school boyfriend had been going there, and then he'd dumped her a week after she'd finalized the decision. Even decades later she remained irritated, with herself, but also with that boyfriend since she found out he'd been planning the split for over a month. Choosing a school based on the weather was a much better way to go about it.

Her phone rang as she tried to decide whether choosing a university based on school colors was a sensible option, forcing her to juggle the mail and mail bag to get her phone out of her pocket. "This is Penelope." She put the brochures into the Cortez's mailbox and headed across the lawn to the next house.

"Hi, this is Susanna Wright."

The voice was familiar but it still took Penelope a second to place her. She let her mind free associate. White Alaskan Husky with a black nose and a chicken allergy... "Jetta's mom." Penelope looked after Jetta a few times a year when Susanna went on vacation.

"Yes! I just got a call from someone who says she found Jetta wandering around almost a mile from the house and I'm two hours away and the lady who found her can't keep her until I get there and..."

"And you need me to go get her," Penelope finished.

"Or if you can't, do you know someone who can?"

"Text me the address. I'll figure it out." She flipped through the stack of mail in her hand and pulled out the bundle for the next house while she hung up and called Jake.

He answered on the third ring. "You didn't find another body, did you?"

"Not yet, but the day is still young. Are you busy?"

There was a long pause. "Am I going to be sorry if I admit I have time?" His voice lowered. "Or is this one of *those* calls."

Penelope grinned as she shoved mail in the next box. "Sadly, no. Maybe later. But one of my clients called. Her dog escaped and she needs someone to go pick her up and bring her home."

"A prisoner transfer. Sure, I can do that."

"Thank you. The dog is Jetta, her owner's last name is Wright." She spelled it for him. "The home address and front door key will be in my binder. I'm assuming there's a gate open and that's how she got out, but maybe take a quick look around when you get there."

Jake cleared his throat. "Please just leave me with the illusion that you don't casually go into houses that someone might be in the process of breaking into."

"Me? I would never. I mean, aside from that one time." He already knew about that time, so she wasn't confessing to anything new. "Jetta's a big white fluffy dog and she's very friendly. I'll text you the address. Call me if you run into any problems." She hung up and went back to checking to see who else was getting interesting mail.

* * *

It was nearly two hours later when she saw a familiar face coming toward her. Two familiar faces, really. Jake was jogging, very slowly, with his leash hand held straight out from his side, and Brutus was eyeing a tree ahead. When the dog saw her, he galloped forward and Jake ran behind him.

Penelope took the two seconds before impact to stow the mail in her hand back in the bag — Brutus generally didn't eat paper, but his drool clung to everything nearby. Then she gave the dog a long hug with butt scratches before looking up at her husband.

"You're right," he said. "He really is a terrible jogging partner."

Penelope brushed some dirt off Jake's shoulder. "He's getting better. Any trouble with Jetta?" He had texted her that the dog was safely home earlier, and she'd passed that along to Susanna, but it had taken him longer than she'd expected.

"Jetta was a perfect angel. The house next door had been broken into and the intruder went into Jetta's backyard to check if he could get into the house before he realized Jetta was there. She went out the dog door into the yard, and the intruder ran off and left the gate open. Then she decided to go on her own walk. The neighbor on the other side got most of it on his security camera." He paused to scratch Brutus's ears. "Apparently not all dogs sound like they're about to come through the door to kill the person on the other side when someone knocks."

"Who's a good little watchdog?" Penelope crooned to Brutus. Not that Brutus would hurt anyone. If someone ignored his growling and barking and went inside, he would undoubtedly treat them like his best friend. She stood up. "I bet Susanna can still get pizza delivered to her place though."

"That thought did cross my mind." He matched her pace as she continued on her route. "In any case, I spent some time talking to the neighbor with the security cameras. He wanted my opinion on whether he should talk to the police about something."

"And you immediately said yes." This was one of the places where they differed. Jake got irritated when people waited to contact the police until things had gone past the point of no return. Penelope thought people called the police for too many stupid things and that could lead to innocent people being hurt. They'd agreed that they were probably talking about different subsets of the population, but it was an argument that resurfaced every so often.

"I had some extra time. I'm retired, you know." He fell behind as he waited for Brutus to finish sniffing, then caught up again. "There was a middle-aged woman sitting in a car watching the house across the street all night. Then in the morning she just drove away."

Penelope winced. "Sounds like someone thinks her husband is cheating on her. Or she's a private investigator working for someone who thinks their spouse is cheating on them. Either way, not a job for the police."

"And yet..."

Penelope shoved another bundle of advertising circulars into the next mailbox. "You think it's a stalking case?"

"What would you say if I told you the car had a bumper sticker for Homespun Harold's Natural Products?"

Penelope stopped walking. "When was this?"

"The night Harold died." He smiled at her expression.

"Amelia caught her husband cheating on her. Or was trying to catch him anyhow. No wonder she's been up in arms lately." Then she realized what he was waiting for her to get. "She has an alibi."

"She does. She's on a security camera from about eight thirty at night until seven in the morning. She couldn't have been at her ex-husband's house in the middle of the night."

Penelope didn't have to ask why Amelia hadn't said anything about it. Coming to terms with being cheated on was not a simple process. Presumably she would have come clean if she'd been arrested, though by then the recording proving her innocence might have been erased. "You told Brian?"

"I did."

"And he said 'Thanks, Jake, you're a good friend', right?"

"Yes, though his actual wording included less thanking and more swearing. He's wasted a bunch of time looking through her finances." He craned his neck to look at the lingerie catalog she was about to put in the next mailbox. "I didn't even know they sent those out any more."

Penelope paused to look at the cover. "It all looks really

uncomfortable." She put it in the mailbox and they kept walking. "Maybe Harold was killed by a complete stranger."

"Ah yes, a serial killer who chooses botulism as his weapon."

She'd known how it sounded the second she'd said it, but now she was committed. "You laugh, but has anyone looked? Maybe someone is killing off all the natural food people."

"Because?"

"The most likely reason is that someone gave them carob instead of chocolate as a child."

Jake laughed. "This sounds like a personal grievance."

"Have you ever had it? It tastes *nothing* like chocolate." She selected the next group of envelopes. "If it wasn't a stranger, and it wasn't Amelia, that pretty much leaves Skye and Edward, doesn't it?"

"For all we know, it might have been the next door neighbor who got tired of listening to how he was doing recycling wrong." Jake waited for Brutus to mark another bush. "But it's probably good that Edward has a decent lawyer."

CHAPTER 19

Sitting on the rectory kitchen floor with Spot the next morning, Penelope heard Jake's footsteps coming up the stairs. "It's open," she called. When he walked in with another covered platter, she narrowed her eyes. "If you want donuts, just go buy some donuts. There's no need to keep torturing CJ with that sausage."

"I'll have you know that this was a special request." He set the platter down on the table, then turned and pointed. "In the pantry?"

"Top right shelf. They may be getting a little stale by now unless there's a new box."

"Donuts never truly go bad. Do you want one, or would you rather just eat mine?" He grinned at her and put two on a plate, then settled down on the floor next to her. "Did I interrupt deep thoughts?"

"Just thinking about how I could kill you and keep Brutus safe." Penelope broke off a piece of the chocolate donut. It had dried out a bit, but Jake was right; donuts never really did go bad.

"Of course. Did I do something in my sleep last night, or is this a hypothetical?"

"Purely hypothetical."

"Good to know. What have you come up with?"

"If I want it to look like an accident, it gets a lot harder. There's no foolproof method. If I knocked you down the stairs, it's entirely possible you would just be a little bruised. And then you would know I was trying to kill you. It would be far easier for you to kill me."

"Has anyone ever told you that you're extremely morbid some mornings?" He broke off a piece of the same donut. "But you're probably right."

"Strength and size make a difference, as much as I like to pretend they don't. I'd probably have to drug you first if I was going to overpower you, but that would show up if someone was looking for it. I can see why people use poison."

"Except then Brutus would potentially be at risk. I see where you're going with this."

"I mean, Brutus may be a special case. There's always the chance that he would eat the poison by itself before I could feed it to you." Clay figurines had been included in the various non-food items that Brutus had eaten since he'd come to stay with them, so this wasn't an unwarranted fear. "But we'll pretend for the moment that Brutus is slightly better behaved."

Jake took a deep breath and blew it out slowly. "That's going to take some imagination, but I'll try."

"So I know that pretty much anything I give you could also be given to the dog. In fact, it's even *likely* that you'll secretly give it to the dog if it's something you don't like."

"We're really off in the hypotheticals now, because I have loved everything you've made for me." He grinned when she raised one eyebrow. "But for the sake of argument, let's assume that I have been known, from time to time, to dispose of a helping or two of casserole surprise by feeding it to the hypothetically well-behaved dog who is a willing participant in all this."

"It's strange how much you seem to have to qualify that statement, but we'll ignore that for the moment." Penelope broke off a piece of the other donut, sending sprinkles onto the floor. Spot watched them fall but didn't bother to raise her head. "Can you imagine having a dog and still having to sweep crumbs off the floor?"

"No, but I *do* remember a time when I didn't have to mop the floor twice in a row just to get all the drool off it."

Penelope nodded. "I remember that time, too. But back to my point." She paused. "I forgot where I was."

"You were about to poison me, but we were imagining that you were worried that I might feed it to Brutus instead of eating it."

"Right. So I *could* sit there and watch you eat. But that might get weird."

"Certainly after this conversation, if you ever watch me too closely, I'm going to distract you and dump it down the garbage disposal. The real one, not the dog."

"So how do I make sure that you don't feed something to the dog? Killing you is one thing, but only a monster would kill the dog." Penelope used her hand to sweep the sprinkles on the floor into a pile.

"Put it in alcohol? We do make an effort not to let the dog drink too much."

They both sighed at that. Brutus had downed half a six-pack of beer one night before they had woken enough to investigate the crunching metal sounds. Everything had turned out fine, but that had been the beginning of strict rules about leaving cans of food or drink anywhere the dog might be able to get to them.

"In this hypothetical scenario, you are an alcoholic in recovery and you don't drink."

"This hypothetical scenario is oddly specific. But okay. No alcohol. How about something else on the list of things dogs aren't allowed to eat? Do I eat chocolate, or did that disappear along with the beer?"

"That might work." Penelope frowned.

"You don't seem pleased."

"Assuming there's not some unknown stranger with a strong motive and close relationship with Harold, it was probably either Skye or Edward. From the way Skye acted toward Crunch that day, I'm not convinced she would have gone out of her way to keep the dog safe. I haven't seen Edward around dogs, but Esther likes him. I bet Edward would make sure that Crunch wouldn't be harmed."

Jake transferred the plate to his other hand and put his free arm over her shoulders. "This is the real reason why you should leave it to the police. But cheer up, I have a solution for you."

"Unknown stranger? That seems unlikely."

"Even better. In your hypothetical scenario, the goal was to kill me without killing Brutus."

"Yes."

"Change it a little. Pretend you don't care at all if Brutus lives, but you really want to be sure I die. Maybe I have a habit of feeding the food you give me to the dog when you're not looking." He cleared his throat. "In this purely hypothetical situation, of course."

"Of course."

"You know you're only going to get one chance. You need to make it good. So you put the poison in something that you know I won't feed to the dog." He offered her the nearly empty plate of doughnuts. "That way you know I get all of it. Then I die, the dog just happens to survive even though that wasn't your goal, and you live happily ever after."

"Hm. That does work, doesn't it?" She ate the last piece of the chocolate donut. "The only problem is that now I can't narrow it down at all."

"You already have narrowed it down. You just don't have any evidence."

Spot scrambled to her feet and went to the door before Penelope could respond. Jake got up first and she let him pull her to her feet. On cue, the door opened and CJ came in, followed by a younger man sporting the half-sunburned, half-tanned look of a person who had just returned from vacation in a sunnier climate.

CJ's eyes fixed on the still-covered platter on the table. "Excellent! Thank you, Jake." He turned to the man behind him. "Jake was kind enough to agree to make me breakfast with boar sausage again. It really is quite an interesting taste." He started to uncover the platter, then paused. "Where are my manners? Do you know each other? This is Hayden Longyear. He's a specialist at St. Sebastian's. Jake Wheeler was the assistant chief of police —"

"Now retired," Jake added.

"And Penelope Standing was our mayor for a while, and is kind enough to look after Spot when I have other duties."

Hayden turned to Jake. "Are you a hunter?" Penelope couldn't tell if he had immediately dismissed her because he didn't notice women over a certain age or because he only wanted to talk about hunting. "I take a boar hunting trip with my med school buddies at least once every few years."

"Not me, I'm afraid. We just had some sausage in the freezer that a friend brought us."

The doctor's interest in Jake visibly dimmed, which gave Penelope her answer. "Too bad. I'll bring you some meat the next time I go."

Penelope suppressed a groan. At this rate they were never going to be rid of the stuff. "Nice to meet you. We should get going." If they left quickly enough, maybe Hayden would forget about his offer.

CJ waved a hand since his mouth was already full. They waited for him to chew and swallow. "Before you go, can you give Hayden the number of the detective in charge of Harold Stone's murder? He may have some information."

Penelope perked up. Maybe they had found an unknown stranger that would increase the suspect pool.

Jake took out his phone and scrolled through the contacts. "Did you know Harold?"

"Only professionally."

Jake paused in writing down Brian's number on a sheet of paper. "Oncologist?" Hayden nodded. When both CJ and Penelope stared at him, Jake smiled. "It wasn't that great a leap. We knew something had changed recently. Everyone assumed Harold had started drinking again, but cancer would explain it all just as easily."

Hayden pursed his lips, then nodded. "If he's been murdered this is all going to come out anyhow, though I'd appreciate it if you wouldn't say anything to anyone else until I have a chance to tell the police." He picked up one of the sausage rolls. "He had a brain tumor."

Jake finished writing and handed over the slip of paper. "How long did he have?"

Hayden frowned, though it didn't seem directed at anyone in the room. "Without treatment, he was probably looking at least another three to six months, maybe longer, though it all depended on how fast it grew. There was always the chance that the tumor could grow into a vessel and cause a bleed that would kill him sooner."

"And with treatment?"

"If he'd been willing to treat it, there was every chance he could have been cured. The tumor itself was benign." He sounded angry.

Penelope understood now. "But Harold wouldn't treat it because chemotherapy isn't natural."

"It would have been radiation, but yes, that was the problem. Completely illogical. By the time I saw him, he wasn't rational about that sort of thing, and nothing I said could convince him. Maybe if I'd seen him when he first started having headaches…"

Penelope shook her head. "Unless the tumor started growing decades ago, that was just Harold being Harold." She had to admit to herself that she was reluctantly impressed with Harold's commitment to his ideals, even in the face of death.

"I finally got him to agree to fill a prescription for his headaches, so I thought maybe I was making some progress. But then I came back from vacation to find that someone had killed him. What a waste."

Penelope met Jake's gaze. She had the feeling that Hayden was more upset that he wouldn't be able to cure the cancer than the loss of life. "Other than the headaches, was he having any symptoms?" When the doctor frowned at her, she gave a half-shrug. "Even his family seems to have been convinced he had started drinking again. I'm just curious why."

"He had started showing some mild issues with balance, especially when he was tired. I talked to him about how he would need support soon, but he refused to tell his family. That didn't surprise me too much, though, since he still downplayed his symptoms, even to me."

"A lot of people find it easier to pretend something isn't happening than deal with it."

Both CJ and Jake looked as if they wanted to argue with that statement, but Hayden nodded. "It's a common problem,

But I think his disease was progressing to the point where he wouldn't have been able to ignore it much longer." Hayden turned to Jake. "Before I forget, I have some boar steaks in my freezer. They're a little on the strong side, but you might like them if you enjoy the sausage."

Penelope fled before she could find out how much freezer space was going to be devoted to nearly inedible meat.

CHAPTER 20

By the time Penelope had finished her other pet sitting duties and headed over to Esther's place for lemonade and information, it was late afternoon and she knew her friend would have already heard about Harold's brain tumor. CJ and Esther had been friends for longer than Penelope had been alive, and they were both interested in people.

Esther opened the door and led the way back to the kitchen. "You know Edward, of course, and this is Tweetie."

Penelope realized that she'd been assuming Edward's fiancée would either be a hardened survivor of underaged partying and tabloid attention — based on who her mother was — or a frivolous pleasure-seeker — based on her name — but the person she found in front of her appeared to be a shy young woman with her dark hair pulled back in a quick ponytail. Flecks of white paint covered her worn jeans and t-shirt. She looked both capable and kind.

Tweetie stood up to shake her hand. "Sorry about the mess." She rubbed at the paint on her knuckle. "I promised my parents I would finish the fence along the driveway this week, and I always forget how much paint I get all over myself."

Esther poured out a glass of lemonade for Penelope. "Have a seat and help with this puzzle. I got the center done this morning, but everything else is the same color and I don't have the patience. I'm trying to make sure all the pieces are here before I add it to the rose garden auction."

Penelope watched as Edward picked up a piece that to her eye looked like every other piece on the table. He reached across the table and confidently slotted it in place.

Tweetie gave her a wry grin. "Edward is the only one making progress. Esther and I have just been talking."

Edward's hands didn't stop moving. "They're trying to make me feel better about yelling at my father when he was dying from a brain tumor."

Penelope picked up a piece and tried to fit it in place. Only after she held it there did she realize there was a slight difference in the intensity of black across the thousand piece puzzle. "But you didn't know he was dying from a brain tumor, did you?" She put the piece back down.

"Does that matter?" He picked up the piece she had just relinquished, and put it in the opposite corner where it fell in place with an audible click. "I should have known something was wrong."

Penelope picked up another piece. "He knew he was sick and he didn't tell you. If he was expecting you to be psychic about his illness, he deserved what he got." After Esther raised her head, Penelope listened to the words she'd just said. "Not being murdered, of course. Nobody deserves that. I meant not having you treat him like he was ill."

Edward took the piece from her fingers and added it in the corner next to him. "I guess. Skye said he didn't tell her either."

Penelope saw a grimace pass over Tweetie's face when

Edward mentioned his sister, but Tweetie didn't say anything. She decided to push a little bit. "I'm surprised Skye didn't guess something was wrong. It would be hard to hide something like that in such a small shop all day."

"Skye just thought he had started drinking."

"Speaking of the shop, I hadn't been in there in a while. It's changed quite a bit, hasn't it? I took a soap making class."

Esther put down the puzzle piece she was holding. "Oh good. Maybe you can teach me. I was thinking about taking that class but it's a bit out of my price range."

Penelope drew in a breath as she thought about the bars curing in the garage. "I don't know if I'm really the best person for that. Mine didn't turn out so great."

Tweetie pushed a couple pieces toward Edward. "I wonder if Skye will keep having classes there after everything is settled."

"Why wouldn't she? They must be fairly lucrative. It's not just the cost of the classes. She was selling molds and everything else related to it, and that stuff isn't cheap."

One side of Tweetie's lip curled. "The only reason Skye kept going with the soap classes for so long is that Harold couldn't handle the scents. They made his headaches worse. He had to change the dish soap he'd been using his entire life because it had a lemon scent." When Edward shifted next to her, she squeezed his hand. "Heaven knows, there was no love lost between your father and me, but Skye knew exactly what she was doing. She didn't want him working in the shop all day, so she made sure he wouldn't be."

"It was *his* shop," Edward said, but it sounded like it was an argument that they'd had before and he was just going through the motions.

"It may have started out that way, but Skye has been making all the decisions for at least the last six months."

Tweetie gazed at Edward and fell silent, but she looked worried.

"I'm no help with this thing." Penelope put down the puzzle piece she was holding and stood up. "The cats are calling." She headed back the hallway toward the cats' room and wasn't surprised when Tweetie made an excuse and followed her.

Tweetie pushed the door almost closed. "He still doesn't understand how much danger he's in," she said in a quiet voice. "The police think it must have been one of the family, which leaves two women who have never even had a speeding ticket, and Edward, who has an arrest record that started when he was fifteen."

"It's worse than that. Amelia has an alibi for the entire night." One of the tabbies leaped into Penelope's arms, and she handed him off to Tweetie so she could start scooping the litter boxes.

"I could have told you, if one of those three was going to plan to kill someone, it would be Skye every time. Amelia might confess just to protect one of her kids, but she shuts down before she gets angry enough to do anything. And Edward doesn't plan *anything*. I'm not sure he can."

That last bit made sense to Penelope, but she couldn't imagine it was a defense he'd be able to use in court. "If it was Skye, the trick is going to be proving it. She seems very organized."

"That's an understatement. Is there a second scoop somewhere? I could help instead of just standing here."

Penelope flashed a smile over her shoulder. "You're helping just by entertaining the cats. I've usually got two of them climbing on me at this point." She moved to the next box. "Assuming Skye has hidden her tracks well, it might be easier to attack the problem by finding her motive. Why would she want to kill her father?"

Tweetie groaned. "Anyone who ever met Harold wanted to kill him. Even I wanted to kill him, and I was only ever around him a few times."

"Yes, but why now? It sounds like she had nearly shoved him out of the shop. And even if he hadn't confided in her about the tumor, I find it hard to believe she wouldn't have known he was sick."

"She just thought he had started drinking."

"Does that make sense, though? It's not like Harold had ongoing lapses in sobriety. As far as I can tell, he stopped drinking when his kids were young and never drank again. So if he never smelled like alcohol, and had headaches bad enough that he filled a prescription for pain pills so he could get to sleep, why would Skye think he was drinking?"

"But we all thought he was drinking and hiding it..." Tweetie stopped. "Now that I think about it, it might have been Skye who made us think that. She made a couple of comments, months ago, before Edward had noticed anything was wrong. And then it was just easier to fit the facts to the theory when he seemed hungover or unsteady." She sighed. "Edward tried to talk to him about it once, but of course when Harold denied it, we just thought he was hiding his drinking."

Penelope paused to remove the tabby from the box she was trying to scoop. "So Skye probably knew, or at least suspected, he was sick and let everyone else think he was drinking for some reason. The problem is, that makes her the one person who wouldn't bother killing Harold — she knew she could just wait for him to die. In the meantime, she could do anything she wanted at the shop because her father stayed away because of the perfumes. Why bother killing him and messing it all up?"

Silence filled the room, broken only by the sound of the

tabby scratching in the sand of the box Penelope had just cleaned.

Tweetie's voice was tentative when she spoke again. "My dad had lung cancer about ten years ago. Everything turned out okay — he's still in remission — but when he was first diagnosed, the doctors only gave him a thirty percent chance of making it through treatment, so it was really scary, for all of us. The day after his diagnosis, he sat down with his lawyers and made sure his will was current and everything was set up so my mom didn't have to worry about anything if he died."

"Putting his affairs in order." Penelope sat on her heels and turned toward Tweetie. "Maybe that's it. Maybe he was going to change his will, and Skye knew about it."

"Except it sounds like Harold had known about the tumor for months. He'd have had all kinds of time to change things."

"Your dad's reaction has skewed your perspective a bit." Penelope finished scooping the last box and stood up. "Your dad got diagnosed, set up a treatment plan, and then got everything ready in case things didn't work out. That's the rational response, of course, but most people aren't rational. Harold certainly wasn't. Harold got diagnosed, and immediately went into denial. Knowing him, he ordered some extra herbs and tried meditating the tumor away."

Tweetie snorted at that last part, but nodded. "That sounds like something he would do."

"Right? Except a few months went by and his headaches were getting worse. He filled a prescription for pain pills. That's a sea change. His oncologist thought he might be getting to the point where he allowed treatment. If he was starting to accept the diagnosis, maybe he had started thinking about putting the rest of his affairs in order."

The tabby moved to the last box and started digging while they thought about it.

"So the big family meeting the next day might have been to tell everyone he was sick," Tweetie said slowly. "But it could also have been…"

"To announce that he'd changed his will," Penelope finished for her. "But with Skye running everything, it seems like he'd be more likely to change it to give everything to her." She remembered what Moira had said. "Unless…" She told Tweetie about Moira's hint about financial impropriety happening at the store. "It all depends on whether Harold knew about it. If Harold found out she was stealing from the shop…"

"He would almost certainly change his will. I have no idea how to prove it, though." Tweetie frowned. "Is that cat okay? It's peed in every litter box."

Penelope watched the tabby jump out of the box and push the door open enough so he could leave the room. "That's normal. He does it every time I clean the boxes." She grabbed the broom and started sweeping up the loose sand the cats had tracked around the floor. At the sound, the orange kitten raced in and began attacking the bristles. "The problem is we're making too many assumptions about what might have been going on. As it stands, Skye doesn't have a motive. Would the executor of the will automatically have an accountant look over the books as part of probate? That may be the only proof we can find."

Tweetie's chin lifted. "I can make sure that happens. I just hope we can keep Edward out of jail in the meantime."

CHAPTER 21

*H*arold's house hadn't changed much since she'd last been there — the front garden looked just as overgrown and nothing had moved — but somehow having the door still sealed with crime tape made it feel emptier.

The daylight made her mission both easier and more complicated. Anyone passing by would be able to see her, but who would call the police on a woman looking through windows during the day? In the end, her choice of timing came down to logistics. She didn't know if the police had left any interior lights on, and she didn't think even the most oblivious neighbors would miss someone using a flash at night.

Besides, this way she would be done before she saw Jake at home. He would want to know where she was going, and then he would tell her to leave it to the police.

Penelope ducked behind the same plant to look through the window. Things looked a little different inside. Black fingerprint powder smudged the door jams and clear tracks in the carpet indicated where the crime scene technicians had walked as they examined the rooms for evidence. A layer of dust covered the dining room table.

Penelope held her phone up to the window and took pictures, angling the camera in both directions in order to get everything in the room. She checked how they had come out. The glare from the window couldn't be helped, unless she broke in, and that was a line she wasn't ready to cross. At least, not yet.

She tried to look casual as she headed toward the side area that would let her into the backyard. Maybe the family had asked her to check on the plants. That would only be neighborly. A chime sounded inside the house when she unlatched the gate and opened it, making her jump. She hurried through and closed the gate again.

The skunky odor of marijuana plants was stronger in the backyard, so it wasn't a surprise to see five large healthy plants, each in its own wine barrel container. Harold might have been nearly impossible to get along with in life, but he certainly knew how to grow a pot plant.

The rest of the yard was taken up by raised beds of herbs and vegetables, with narrow pathways of gravel between them, and the plants showed the same evidence of neglect that she'd seen in the front garden. Fruit trees and compost piles lined the back fence. All in all, it looked like a peaceful place to sit and enjoy a morning cup of coffee. Or it would have, if there had been anywhere to sit down. It didn't appear that Harold had spent much time relaxing in his garden.

No photos taken through the kitchen window would be as good as the ones she'd seen on Brian's computer, so she went to the French doors that led into the living room. Disorder reigned, but it looked like that was how Harold had left it. One wall was taken up by bookshelves, a mix of non-fiction with no obvious order to them that she could see.

When he'd run out of space to file them vertically, he'd stacked the remainder on top of the other books. The over-flow was distributed in piles on every available surface and continued on the floor. Penelope held her phone to the window and started taking pictures again, hoping to include all the books in her new photo album. If she could figure out Harold's filing system later, she might be able to determine if something had been disturbed.

She hoped the evidence she was looking for wasn't something in the upstairs bedrooms. There wasn't a nearby tree or even a convenient trellis for her to climb. Next time she'd have to remember to bring a ladder.

She set the phone in video mode and scanned the whole room, hoping that it would pick up any areas she had missed with her still photos.

A woman's voice cut into the silence. "Skye! How are you?"

Penelope's phone smacked into the window, and she froze, her heart racing. If Skye was here, there was no way she'd be able to make it out of the yard without being seen, not with the alarm on the side gate.

The woman's voice continued. "I wonder if you'd made a decision about that thing we talked about last week."

Penelope exhaled, localizing the voice and realizing what was going on. The woman next door was standing in her yard, talking to Skye on the phone. Were the gaps between the fence slats wide enough for her to see Penelope? Obvi-ously she hadn't yet, or she'd be calling the police or just yelling for help.

Penelope shoved her phone into her pocket and started edging back toward the gate. Luckily the gate was on the opposite side of the house from where this woman was carrying on her high-decibel conversation. After Penelope had rounded the corner with no sign of being spotted, she trotted forward, then stopped with her hand on the gate.

If she opened the gate, the chime would sound in the house. It was loud enough that the neighbor would be able to hear it. Maybe it would be better to climb over the gate. She pushed the garbage bin closer to the fence and climbed on top.

Harold had opted for the smaller size garbage bin, and while she admired his frugality and commitment to generating as little waste as possible, the small bin wasn't nearly as sturdy as the larger bins. The lid bowed alarmingly as she moved from her knees to her feet.

She grabbed the top of the gate, pivoted, and lifted one foot. All she needed to do was get one sneaker against the outside of the gate, and then she'd be able to swing the other leg over and hop down.

The garbage bin lid buckled, and her center of gravity fell abruptly. Penelope went sideways, and her hands slipped off the top of the gate. For an instant she thought she was going to go headfirst into the concrete walkway, but reflex and luck let her catch herself upside down, with her knees hanging over the top of the fence.

Her phone slipped out of her pocket and clattered to the ground.

Penelope took a breath and tried to look at the bright side as the blood rushed to her head. Other than a few splinters, she wasn't injured. More importantly, nobody had seen this. She curled up to grab the top of the gate, then kicked her feet up and over. One heel got stuck on the first try, but she kicked up again and then dropped down to her feet.

There. She was no longer in the backyard, and nobody had seen her less-than-graceful dismount. Penelope brushed her hands off on her shirt, picked up her phone, and bolted.

* * *

Jake reached over to move the video backward. They were curled together on the couch in their usual positions, Jake propped up by the corner and Penelope leaning back against him with her computer on her lap, and Brutus on her feet. "My second favorite part is the look you have on your face here when you think your foot is stuck."

Only after she'd made it home and uploaded everything to her computer had Penelope realized that she hadn't stopped the video when the neighbor had started talking, so there was muffled audio of her escape until the phone had fallen to the ground. It had landed in a way that kept her legs in the frame as she hung upside down, and then her whole body was visible as she worked to free herself.

"I'm glad you find this entertaining. What's your favorite part?"

"That glimpse of skin visible at your waistline when you're hanging by your knees."

"You can only see an inch of my stomach."

"Yes, but it's a very sexy stomach."

On the screen, there was whispered swearing as she worked to free herself. "I think you're missing the point. I wanted to look at the living room."

Jake paused and rewound. "And here I thought you didn't know some of those words." He tapped the play button again.

Penelope lifted her head so she could look him in the eye. "Do you want to hear them again?"

He grinned and clicked the button to close the video. "Don't erase it. I want to make some GIFs."

Penelope made a mental note to be sure that she deleted the original copy on her phone at the same time she wiped it from her computer. She brought up the first picture of the living room. "Harold was a reader. That much is obvious.

And it looks like he bought books and then kept them for reference."

"Or kept them for kindling. That place looks like a firetrap."

Penelope zoomed in and scanned the shelves. Even with the pixelation, dusty window, and poor lighting, she recognized a lot of the books. One section had the counterculture classics. *Silent Spring* was there, and a few other environmental texts. "I wonder if he bought his copy of *Steal This Book*?" Then it slipped into fiction from a similar time period. Hunter S. Thompson had half a shelf to himself. Hardbound copies of Jack Kerouac took up the rest of the space. "Half this stuff was published before he was born."

"A lot of books were." Now that he didn't have a video of Penelope flailing upside down in front of him, Jake's attention had slipped back to the golf tournament on television.

"Yes, but there's hardly anything written after 1980. That's weird, right? There's almost nothing from when he was an adult."

Jake didn't turn his head. "It looks like the room hasn't been decorated since that time either."

Penelope panned around, looking at the different topics on the book shelves. One whole section was devoted to natural food cookbooks and reprints of old English gardening manuals. There was a shelf on natural pest control, and another two held what looked like years of organic gardening magazines. Only one shelf looked like it held newer publications, and she flipped through her pictures until she found the one with the clearest image.

Aside from the hefty computer programming manual — for a computer that hadn't been sold in at least a decade — most of the books looked like they had been bought for business-related purposes. A small business tax guide stood next to a book on advertising, which leaned against... "Why would he store a bound version of *The Anarchist's Cookbook* with the business books?"

Jake raised an eyebrow and looked at the screen. "Who buys *The Anarchist's Cookbook* anymore? You can watch videos online for free." He turned his attention back to the television.

Penelope looked at the gap *The Anarchist's Cookbook* didn't completely fill. She scanned the tower of books leaning against the recliner. A lumpy couch and an unpadded wooden bench offered other seating alternatives in the room, but based on how much of the clutter it had attracted, Penelope was fairly certain the armchair had been where Harold spent most of his time at home. The books he'd been reading recently suggested a theme — all but one had "herb" or "healing", or both, in the title. That final one, though...

"Aha!"

A round of quiet clapping came from the speakers. Jake looked down at her computer. "You found something worth falling over a fence for?"

"I didn't fall."

His lips twitched. "Can we watch the video again? I think I might be able to point out a few things to you."

"Later. Look at this." She used the mouse to draw his attention to the stack of books next to Harold's recliner.

Jake squinted. *"The Healing Way, Natural Healing...* Wait, wasn't that a Marvin Gaye song?"

"No, that was *Sexual Healing*. That's a totally different thing. Look at the book below that."

"Writing Your Own Will." He leaned back and stopped squinting. "That makes sense. He had a brain tumor."

"Yes, but nobody found a new will. Maybe that's what the killer came back for that night."

Jake gave her a dubious look. "Or maybe he hadn't gotten around to writing another one yet and it never existed."

"That's also possible, I guess." She closed her laptop. "I still think it suggests that he was planning on changing his will. And that gives someone a motive."

They watched the camera pan over the course and then narrow in on the ball bouncing once on the green.

"I think you're probably right. But there's a huge difference between an assumption based on a book in a stack next to a chair and a fact that will hold up in court."

"If I could have figured out how to get inside, maybe I could have found something. Maybe he left notes in the margins."

"Do me a favor? Try not to get picked up on B&E until at least one week has gone by since the retirement party."

"Just you wait. Soon you'll be joining me in my life of crime."

"I'm not sure I'm flexible enough. Would I be required to flip backward over fences, or could I just go through the gate?"

"I was trying to keep it from making noise, but I'm pretty sure you have the upper body strength to have just jumped over it without getting too fancy."

"Ah yes, fancy was definitely the word I was looking for." He reached over to open her laptop and started the video running again. The dark screen suddenly gave way to a confusing blur of motion as the phone fell, accompanied by her muffled swearing, and then the frame stabilized, with a clear shot of Penelope hanging upside down by her knees. "Very fancy."

Penelope snapped the laptop closed again and set it down on the floor. "You're just jealous of my reflexes."

"Definitely."

"Is this tournament live?"

"I'm sure I could catch the highlights later if you have

something else in mind." He paused. "You *are* talking about going upstairs, right, not breaking into Harold's house?"

"I love that you aren't sure." She pulled her feet out from under Brutus, and the dog lifted his head. "If you take care of the lights, I'll get something out of the freezer to keep your dog occupied."

CHAPTER 22

With no mail delivery duties and only the regular amount of pet sitting clients to take care of, Penelope had agreed to help with a training exercise for Brutus. She had hidden five boxes along a predetermined route, each with a scent lure inside. They'd gone with *Harold's Own* this time — Penelope hoped the dog could distinguish it from all the other plant smells along the way. Jake wasn't supposed to have any idea where she had hidden the lures so he couldn't inadvertently communicate that to Brutus through body language. Now Penelope was trailing behind them, close enough to call to them if they went too far past one of the boxes, but far enough away that Brutus wasn't likely to read anything into her movements. She was also responsible for picking up what was left of the boxes after Jake got them away from Brutus.

Brutus had found the first box easily enough, but it had taken a frustrating three minutes of trying to keep him from eating the cardboard before the dog sat down, his signal that he had found something. Penelope had caught up to them after Brutus had found the box, knowing that Jake might need a little support. "Just be patient," she'd advised after Jake had pulled the box out of the dog's mouth for the fourth time. That was the moment Brutus sat down, and she'd joined in on giving treats and praise.

"I think he just sat down because he was tired of standing."

"Probably. That's okay, though. At some point he'll make the connection." Penelope thought Brutus would pick it up pretty quickly — he was strongly motivated by food — but she didn't say that. If the dog didn't link the two actions right away, she didn't want Jake to worry he'd done something wrong. She put what was left of the box in the trash bag she'd brought along for the purpose. "Off you go."

Their path covered half a mile, which gave enough space between each box that the scents shouldn't overlap much, but not so much distance that Brutus would forget about what he was supposed to be doing. At least that was the hope. If it didn't go well, Penelope was prepared to suggest they finish early.

Brutus got distracted by a dog on the other side of the street and missed the second box completely. Penelope waited until they were two houses beyond it and dialed Jake's number. "Turn around and come back this way for a bit."

She heard him sigh before he cut the connection.

On the second pass, with no extra distractions, Brutus found the box, and this time it only took him thirty seconds before he sat down. Penelope walked up as Brutus was gobbling treats. "See, he's almost figured it out already."

"Yeah, as long as there's nothing around to distract him."

"He hasn't figured out the rules to the game yet. Once he knows he gets treats when he finds stuff, he'll concentrate harder." She put the soggy cardboard into her bag. She waved them off and waited for them to get far enough ahead that she could follow.

The route she had chosen took them downtown, which was a bit of an extra challenge with all the different smells, but at least they were doing this in the morning before lunchtime, when there would be a lot less food scattered on the ground for Brutus to find.

Penelope looked along the pavement. Security cameras covered most of the street and the parking areas, including the front door of Homespun Harold's All-Natural Emporium. That had given Skye her alibi. She had been rearranging stock in the store nearly the entire night, or so she claimed. There was security video that showed her going through the front door with her dinner in the early evening. The next time the door was opened was just ten minutes before she'd shown up at her father's house the morning Penelope had found the body.

Penelope looked up and identified the camera that had taken the footage. Unless Skye had some sort of secret hacking skills that had corrupted the video, Penelope couldn't see how she'd left through the front.

The third scent box was hidden under the insulating blanket locked onto a water meter, and Jake was clearly missing the connection when Brutus sat down in front of it. He was still looking around when Penelope called him. "Quick, give him a bunch of treats!" Dog training was all about timing, and they were quickly moving past the window on this one.

By the time she caught up to them, Brutus had eaten his treats and Jake had found the box. He handed it to her as she walked up. "It only took three tries before he figured it out and I messed it up." His voice was rueful, but there was also a bit of pride.

"Don't feel bad. Dog training is always ten percent about the dog and ninety percent about the handler. Our dog is a genius."

"What I find interesting is that of all the routes you could have set, we went past the front of Harold's shop and now we're going down the alley behind it."

"I wanted to look at the security cameras. How hard is it to hack into them and change the footage?"

"A lot harder than it looks on television." He sighed. "I hate to encourage this sort of thing, but let's go look at the alley."

Penelope watched them walk away. As much as Jake claimed she should leave everything to the police, he was walking with more purpose in his stride than he had during the earlier parts of the exercise. She followed man and dog around the corner, and then into the alley behind the shops.

All of the businesses had fenced-in spaces behind them, a legacy of the age when the row of buildings had been constructed. The bars and restaurants had created outdoor areas for customers to enjoy during nice weather. Most of the other businesses had filled the space with storage sheds, or made small areas for employees to take breaks out of the sight of customers. Skye had turned hers into an area to teach crafts and mix dangerous chemicals.

Just when Penelope thought she was going to have to call Jake and tell him to turn around, Brutus doubled back and sat down in front of the bush where she had wedged the box. This time it only took Jake a moment to notice. By the time Penelope had caught up to them, Brutus had eaten his treats and was lying on his belly in the shade.

"The two of you are doing great." She reached down to tug on Brutus's ear and feed him a treat. "So what do you think?"

Jake scanned the street. "Out front the cameras are higher up and the coverage overlaps because the city installed them. Back here, though..." He pointed. "That camera is going to catch anyone going through the back gate, but the way it's installed there under the eaves, I bet the door to the shop is blocked."

Penelope followed his finger. "So Skye might have been able to get onto the patio without being on camera, but she couldn't get out the gate."

Jake's attention went to the business on the side closest to the door. "She could have gone over the fence into the restaurant patio and then gone out their gate, as long as it wasn't locked."

"But then she would have ended up on their security footage."

Jake nodded. "That only matters if someone looks at it. Which they might not." He walked closer to the fence. "But I think if I was trying to sneak out, I'd go out the door and hug this side and then climb over the fence." His lips twitched.

Penelope narrowed her eyes at him. "If you start making fence climbing jokes, I'm going to make sure the next training exercise passes behind a row of overflowing dumpsters."

"I wouldn't dream of it." He took out his phone, looked at it, and smiled.

Penelope reached out and tilted the screen so she could see it. The screen lock picture showed her hanging upside down from the gate. "How did you get that? I erased everything while you were still asleep this morning."

"Insomnia occasionally has its benefits."

Penelope shook her head and went to look at the fence. Made entirely of wood, it looked like coarsely woven cloth, with 4x4" posts providing the warp and gently curving 1x6" slats as the weft. The end result was attractive and left areas that could be used as toeholds for climbing. "I could probably make it over this if I really had to."

Jake held his phone out in front of him. "Hang on. Let me make sure I have the right angle for this before you start."

"Very funny." She walked back to him. "The problem is that even if we can prove that she *could* have done it, that doesn't actually show that she *did* do it."

"Don't think I didn't notice how this suddenly turned into *our* project, but ignoring that for the moment, I agree. Her car was parked out front, so we know she didn't drive it to her father's house, but the house is in easy walking distance from here." He turned to face the general direction of Harold's house. "There aren't any intersection cameras she would have needed to avoid. The area is all low-traffic residential. Most residential security cameras aren't aimed toward the sidewalk. It would give too many false motion alerts."

"As well as being a violation of privacy for anyone walking by," Penelope added, catching his eye.

Jake held up his hands in surrender. "I'll let you take that up with the courts. I'm just talking about practical aspects here." He looked at the camera covering the back gate of Harold's shop again. "I'll mention the fence climbing possibility to Brian, and suggest someone check the restaurant's security footage just in case." He used his toe to nudge Brutus's rear end. "You snoozing on the job there, buddy? Let's go. Find it!"

Penelope waited for them to get a little farther ahead. The back door of Homespun Harold's All-Natural Emporium opened, and through the gaps in the woven slats, she saw Skye walk on a diagonal path to get to one of the sheds, but her face was turned toward Penelope, as if she knew exactly where she was standing. She had a little frown on her face.

As she tried to decide if Skye really knew she was there, Penelope heard a voice she recognized. Walking around the corner, Lorna Harvey was having an animated conversation with the woman next to her.

Penelope sprinted after Jake and Brutus.

*a*fter a week of parties and dead bodies, Penelope had an evening at home alone, and she intended to make the most of it. Not that she didn't enjoy her evenings with her husband, but Jake didn't particularly like the taste of anchovies, so she reserved her evenings of romantic comedies while eating anchovies on toast for those times when she knew he wasn't going to be around. This evening he had gone out with friends for wine, burgers, and bocce at a bar two counties over. She'd been invited, but she'd been to those outings before, and no matter how hard they tried not to, everyone reverted to talking about work within fifteen minutes.

She'd just sat down on the couch with her dinner, Brutus sitting on her feet, when Esther called. Penelope gave Brutus a glare as he tried to wiggle his frame closer to her plate even as she answered the phone. "Hi, Esther. Is everything okay?"

"No. Or yes, I'm fine, but Tweetie thinks they're going to arrest Edward in the morning."

Penelope put her bare feet on Brutus's shoulders to keep him from climbing into her lap. "Why?"

"They found an empty pill bottle with Harold's name on it in his car. And then they found one of Harold's old diaries concealed under his porch."

"That's not good." She considered the news. "Didn't they already search his car and his house while they had him in for questioning?"

"They did, but they're saying he was hiding the pills somewhere else until it was safe to keep them in his car, and they might not have searched under the porch the first time."

That was one way to look at it, and she had to admit it was logical if you first assumed that Edward had done it. If you were pretty sure he hadn't... "You said it was one of the older diaries? From when?"

"I think about five years ago."

Penelope thwarted another attempt by the dog to creep forward. "Which was right before Edward got serious about sobriety, wasn't it? So if it's not just information about the business in there, it's going to have a list of everything Harold thought Edward had stolen from him. In other words, it's going to paint Edward in the worst possible light."

"Yes. It's obvious Skye planted it. At least, it's obvious to me. Why would Edward keep the diary with the worst information about himself?"

Penelope thought Skye might have misstepped with that one as well. "I think I must have rattled her this morning." She told Esther about how Skye might have seen her examining the security cameras. "Except I don't see why she would be any more worried just because we realized her alibi might not be as good as it looked. It still doesn't give us any proof that she did it. This feels like panic."

Brutus had decided they were playing a new game, and lunged forward. She used her feet to push him sideways, and he landed on the floor and bowed down, then zipped around the couch and bowed again.

"Or she's buying time, for some reason." Esther sounded worried. "I know this can all be explained away, but it bothers me. If Edward didn't have a good lawyer, they probably would have charged him already, and with his history…"

Penelope jumped to her feet before Brutus could leap on her. "Let me think about it tonight. I'll call you in the morning." She tossed the phone on the couch and used her free hand to take a bite of toast as she headed toward the kitchen. "Did you not get enough exercise today? Let's go for a walk."

She always thought better when she was moving, and if their walk took them past Homespun Harold's All-Natural Emporium so she could figure out what they had done to spook Skye into planting evidence… Well, dogs liked to walk all over the place.

She crammed the last bit of toast in her mouth and picked up Brutus's bag of treats.

CHAPTER 24

*P*enelope spent a lot of time on foot in every part of town. Middle of the night walks were usually peaceful because nobody was around; early morning walks held a sense of purpose, with everyone exercising before the start of another work day; daytime walks were often business-like affairs, especially since some days she rushed from one client to another, trying to fit them all in.

Early evening walks weren't her favorite. With everyone racing around to get errands done after work, there was more traffic, yet it was dark enough that pedestrians were harder to see. On top of that, evening walks downtown involved going by people at bars, and Penelope wasn't a big fan of questions by groups of tipsy men on the sidewalk.

Luckily, with Brutus by her side all anyone ever wanted to talk about was the dog. Between jokes about having a dog as big as a horse, and comments about how much it must cost to feed a dog that size, hardly anyone ever said anything inappropriate. Brutus was excellent protection merely by convincing everyone that they should only think about dogs for a while. Penelope appreciated that.

Having such a memorable dog did make it a little hard to be unnoticed. Homespun Harold's All-Natural Emporium was still open. Inside the shop, Skye was saying something about the different kinds of looms that she could special-order if necessary. Penelope planned to walk quickly past and then head around to the alley to see what she and Jake had missed that morning while they were focused on security cameras.

That plan fell apart when Brutus got near the door and sat down, then stared at her, obviously waiting for something. It took Penelope a long moment to remember the scent tracking game. Brutus had detected the same scent coming from the shop. It made sense. That was where Penelope had bought the essential oil in the first place. Harold may have even made it right there in the shop. But it was still an impressive feat.

Impressive or not, Brutus sitting down next to the shop door was inconvenient for Penelope's attempt at stealth. She grabbed treats out of the bag, shoved them at Brutus, and got him moving again, but she was pretty sure there was a moment when Skye paused during her sales speech.

They were almost at the corner when a new complication popped up.

"Mayor Standing! Yoohoo! Mayor Standing!"

Penelope didn't turn to look, but it sounded like Lorna Harvey was on the other side of the street. If Penelope stayed where she was, she'd be stuck for at least an hour. She ducked around the corner and told herself that hiding from Lorna was a good thing. With Lorna's history of heart disease, it would be better if she didn't get worked up by yelling at Penelope.

She glanced back, and when she didn't see Lorna behind her, pulled Brutus into a jog and then turned into the alley behind the shops

The alley wasn't as well lit as the Main Street, with fixtures from individual businesses illuminating nearby patches. The restaurants and bars were open, though, so there were more people on foot. If Brutus hadn't been with her, Penelope could have ducked into one of the restaurant patios and headed through the business back to the street. As it was, she paused behind the bulk of a commercial dumpster, wrinkling her nose at the smell of rancid grease and rotting vegetables. Brutus stood on his hind legs to sniff at the lid in delight.

Her phone rang. "Hi Jake. How's bocce going?"

"Not great. A bachelorette party was using the next court and we lost half our players to them. I finally gave up. I'm on my way home. Why are you whispering?"

"Lorna Harvey."

"Again?"

"She's everywhere. It's uncanny."

A pause ensued. "When you say she's everywhere... You wouldn't happen to mean near Harold's shop downtown, would you?"

The problem with marriage was that a spouse might know you as well as you knew yourself. "Brutus wanted to go for a walk."

Jake took that as the confirmation it clearly was. "Penelope..."

"Esther called earlier. They did another search of Edward's car and house and found some things that weren't there before. I just wanted another look to see if I could figure out why Skye panicked when she saw us looking at the back of the shop."

There was another long pause, which gave her enough time to remember that she hadn't mentioned Skye coming out of the shop after Jake and Brutus had started searching for the next scent box.

"I'll get Brian to come over in the morning and you can lay it all out for him, okay? But will you please just get away from there? If she really is panicking and planting evidence, there's no way to tell what she might do."

"Fine. I need to go home and take a shower anyway. I'm hiding from Lorna behind one of those huge dumpsters and I think the smell is starting to cling to my clothes." She looked at Brutus, who was making a serious effort to shove his nose under the locked lid. "I may have to leave your dog behind, though. I think he found heaven."

"I'll be home in fifteen minutes."

"See you there." Penelope hung up and poked Brutus in the shoulder with one finger. "It's locked. You're not going to get in there. Let's go home."

Brutus gave up with a mournful sigh and they headed toward the end of the alley.

"Mayor Standing!" Lorna was right behind her.

Penelope stopped walking, closed her eyes, and sighed. There was no escaping it. She forced a smile on her face and turned. "Hi, Mrs. Harvey. How are you doing this evening?"

"I'm fine, but I think you need to get your hearing checked. I've been calling your name for five minutes now." She took a few steps closer.

Penelope got ready to jump forward and catch Lorna if she tripped or fainted. "I was on the phone with my husband."

Lorna sniffed. "You picked an odd place to stay. Are you having back problems? You seem to be crouching." She gestured Penelope away from the dumpster, and stopped near the back gate of Homespun Harold's All-Natural Emporium.

The gate wasn't latched. Penelope edged over so she could see through the gap. "You know I'm not the mayor anymore, right?"

Lorna slapped the fence for emphasis. "That's what I've been trying to get in touch with you about. I have some ideas for your reelection campaign."

Momentarily forgetting all about Skye, Harold, and the shop she'd been trying to peek into, Penelope stared at Lorna. "My what?"

"Your reelection campaign. I know we didn't always see eye to eye when you were in office, but at least I trusted you were *trying* to do the best thing for our town. The people that are in there now just want to be able to build whatever they want so they can make a profit and leave, and they haven't given any thought to the infrastructure that needs to be added in order to handle that type of growth."

Penelope wondered if the dumpster fumes were making her hallucinate. She'd made this argument during council meetings, but nobody wanted to hear about long-term issues when so many short-term problems would be solved by construction jobs and businesses that might be lured to the area with the promise of abundant housing. Penelope's questions about waste treatment capacity and traffic patterns were talked over. With the rest of the council united against her, Penelope had the power to be an irritant, but not much else.

And now here was someone she'd thought was out to get her, offering to be an ally.

"I haven't decided if I'll be running again," she admitted. "It all depends on who else is in the race." If someone suitable was willing to take on the public role, Penelope was quite happy to keep working in the background.

Lorna huffed. "Just don't leave it too late. A campaign without deep pockets requires a lot more time to build momentum and gain visibility." She dipped her chin. "Good night, Ms. Standing."

Penelope watched her walk away, still half-expecting her

to trip and fall, but Lorna navigated the root-torn asphalt with ease until she disappeared around the corner.

With a quick shake of her head, Penelope brought her thoughts back to the present. "Pigs may be flying, Brutus. Let's go home before they let loose on us."

That was when she discovered that while she'd been talking to Lorna Harvey, Brutus had taken the opportunity to push open the gate and wander into the patio of Home-spun Harold's All-Natural Emporium. Attached to a six-foot leash, he hadn't made it far, but he was sitting in front of a smaller trash can. Training him using a scent found all over this shop might have been a mistake.

Having finally figured out the rules of the game, Brutus wasn't going to budge until he got his promised treat. Penelope dug in the treat bag, and only after she had given it to the dog did she realize Skye was seated at the table, watching her.

"Sorry. I got distracted and the gate wasn't latched." Penelope waved and didn't meet Skye's eyes, well aware she was adding to her slightly scatterbrained reputation. That reputation was useful at times. "Good night."

"Penelope, right? Have a seat. Maybe you can help."

The smart thing to do would be to pretend she hadn't heard Skye say that. Jake would be home soon and he would be worried if she wasn't there. She should just let Brian figure it all out in the morning.

But there had to be at least fifty people within shouting range. Penelope sat down. "For just a couple of minutes. My husband's on his way home." No, that made it sound as if Jake ruled her movements. "I said I'd meet him there and he gets worried sometimes." That wasn't much better, but it was the best she could do without admitting that Jake was worried about Skye in particular.

"I'll close the gate so you can let your dog loose." Skye got up, pushed the gate closed, and unclipped the leash from Brutus as she spoke. "There's nothing he can get into back here. My father's dog spent a lot of time here." She sat back down behind her notebook.

Penelope glanced at the sheds to make sure they were really closed. Everything that might be a hazard to Brutus would be inside. "How can I help?"

"I'm working on my father's eulogy."

"Ah." Penelope tried to think of a polite response, but her mind was blank. Writing a eulogy for Harold would be a challenge.

Skye laughed. "You see my problem."

"You could focus on his concern for everyone's health."

"See, I knew you'd be able to help." She scribbled in the notebook in front of her on the table. "Can I get you something to drink? Water? A fruit smoothie? I've been working on a new line for the shop to sell."

Sitting in a semi-public place with Skye may have been evidence of questionable decision making, but Penelope wasn't stupid enough to accept any food or drink from her. "No, thanks. I just ate."

Skye grinned, as if she'd heard Penelope's thoughts. "Of course. Hang on a second. I want to grab some water."

Skye went into the building and returned a few minutes later with a bottle of water. She saw Penelope look at the bottle in her hands and laughed. "Yes, yes, plastic is a sign of the devil, but have you ever tasted the water that comes out of these pipes?" She shook her head, sat down, and picked up her pen. "Anything else?" When Penelope didn't speak, Skye indicated the page. "For the eulogy."

Oh, right. "His love for the planet."

"That's perfect." Skye wrote in the notebook. "'He tried to improve everyone's health and the health of the planet' sounds so much better than what I had come up with."

Penelope could leave now while they were both pretending this was nothing more than a eulogy brainstorming session. She could just stand up, say good night, and lead Brutus out of here, and Skye would smile and wave.

And Penelope might never know the truth.

She stayed in her seat. "What had you come up with?"

"I hadn't settled on the final wording yet, but it was something along the lines of 'My father was a poison to everyone around him. He was only happy when he controlled them.'" She shrugged. "You can see why I was having trouble coming up with something that wouldn't make me look bad. Telling the truth at the eulogy is frowned upon."

Penelope had listened to more than a few uncomfortable eulogies over the years, but they had all been given by people who had loved the deceased while not being blind to their faults. Somehow she didn't think that was the case here. "You could have left. With your marketing skills…"

"He *owed* me."

The pleasant look was gone from Skye's face, strong emotion darkening her eyes. For the first time, Penelope thought she was seeing the real Skye.

"First, it was 'there's no money for college because Bear's rehab cost too much, but if you work in the shop for a few years, I'll pay for everything', and then that never happened, but he promised he'd split the business with me. But of course, he always had excuses when I suggested we make it official. After all, we were family. You have to trust your family, right?"

Penelope tried not to react, but she couldn't help wincing.

Skye's rage disappeared in an instant, and the pleasant smile came back. "Sunk cost fallacy, they call it." Her voice had taken on a lofty air. "That's when you've spent so much on something that it's hard to walk away as long as there's some chance of getting it back. Even if that chance is remote.

I knew he was never going to keep his promises, but there was always that chance…" Her lips twisted in a grimace. "He knew all about it. And for him, it was never about the money really. He just wanted someone to keep this damn place running forever." A cunning smile spread over her face. "So I changed it."

Penelope nodded slowly, impressed with the strategy even if she didn't want to be. "If you were chained to him, then he was chained to you as well." Brutus, interested in exploring the other areas of the patio, wandered away, sniffing at the fence where Crunch had presumably left his own calling card. Penelope checked again, but the sheds were closed up, with padlocks keeping them that way. Even Brutus couldn't get past a padlock.

"Exactly! I knew you'd understand." Skye sighed. "I'd say that we'd have been friends under different circumstances, but I probably never would have noticed you."

Penelope tried to decide if that was supposed to be a compliment. Probably not, though she didn't think Skye intended it as an insult either, just a statement of fact.

"Anyhow, by that point he needed me to run the business and he knew it. Nobody wanted to come in so they could listen to him give the same speech about GMOs and pesticides while they bought their vital wheat gluten. Half the people were gluten-free anyhow, and the rest just went to the grocery store. It was cheaper there and they didn't have to deal with him."

"I'm a little surprised it lasted as long as it did."

Skye waved a dismissive hand. "Oh, there's still a group of people who think buying everything from a health food store will make them live forever." Her lips twisted into a smile. "Turns out they're getting old just like everyone else. And eating all the antioxidants in the world won't protect you from skin cancer if you go outside without sunscreen."

She shook her head. "You never bought into all that, did you?"

"Sunscreen, yes, but I never had time to sprout beans and bake my own bread."

"You were one of those moms that brought cupcakes from the store for school parties, weren't you?" When Penelope gave a guilty nod, Skye continued. "I used to be so jealous of those kids. Every year my mother would try to convince the entire class that cupcakes made of sweet potato and carob were just as good as chocolate. Even ten year olds aren't stupid enough to believe that."

"I never really understood the obsession with carob."

Skye laughed. "Me either. Of course, these days chocolate is 'healthy' as long as it's produced by a small company and dark enough that it doesn't seem like dessert. That was one of the few changes in the last twenty years that my father agreed with."

Penelope glanced around to make sure Brutus was behaving himself, but he was still sniffing along the fence line. "So you turned the shop into something he didn't want and started making money."

Skye laughed again. "I targeted those women because they had the most time and disposable income, but after I saw how it was working out... I would have done it for free. They would drive up in their giant cars with their sugary coffees and just... *ignore* him like he didn't matter at all. In his own store!" Her voice held disbelief and pride.

"But they did have money." Moira had suggested there might be financial misdeeds happening. "Let me guess, you figured out a way to take some of that for yourself."

Skye raised one eyebrow and wagged a finger at her. "Trying to get me to incriminate myself is bad form, you know."

"Hypothetically, then. In an alternate timeline, you might

have figured out a way to make more money." Penelope was counting on the fact that Skye had to have been keeping this all to herself for months, if not years. She was probably dying to share it with someone.

Skye looked off into the distance, considering, and Penelope thought her bait wasn't going to work. Then Skye shrugged. "Sure, why not. *Hypothetically*, I might have figured out how to divert some of the money so it didn't show up in the general accounts. My father thought he was an expert at computers because he wrote a program twenty years ago to make an LED blink on and off. But once we got rid of the handwritten ledger, he had no idea what was going on."

Penelope nodded. She'd thought it might be something like that. "He really was stuck in the past."

"You have *no* idea."

From the light coming out of the shop's windows, Penelope could see that Brutus was still sniffing things, so she looked back at Skye. "So you were making extra money —"

"Hypothetically."

"Yes, hypothetically. Why change anything? He was dying anyway." A burst of laughter from the bar's patio reassured her that they weren't alone, but in the darkness with just the light spilling from the shop window, their table felt strangely intimate, a bubble apart from the rest of the town.

"If I'd known that..." Skye scrunched up her face in thought, then shook her head. "Never mind. It wouldn't have changed anything."

"You didn't know?"

"That he had a brain tumor? No, that was a surprise." She looked at Penelope. "I knew *something* was wrong, but he never said anything. I really did think for a while that he'd started drinking again."

"You didn't ask?"

"I didn't care. He was spending less time at the shop. I

wasn't about to complain. In retrospect, that may have been a mistake."

"In what way?" Penelope didn't think Skye regretted her lack of humanity. There had to be a more practical reason.

"I thought he was just showing signs of early onset dementia compounded by depression. Both run in the family, you know." She waved her hand again, a dim movement in the darkness. "Not everything fit, but the sudden mood changes, the unpaid bills stacking up... I thought I'd be able to have him declared unfit by the end of the year, dump him in some facility, and never have to deal with him again. After he died, I could sell everything and move to Hawaii." Something in Penelope's face made her stop. "That sounds cold, doesn't it? Sometimes I forget that I shouldn't be so honest."

"It sounds like you had a plan, anyhow. Could you really sell the shop and make enough to retire?"

Skye laughed and glanced toward the lighted shop windows. "The inventory probably wouldn't even cover the monthly rent. I might be able to sell the crafting side to someone, but I'd probably have to stay on to help run it. No, the shop itself is almost worthless. It's the licensing deal that's really worth the money. Even then, it's not worth all that much, but it would be enough to support one person fairly comfortably, even after renegotiating so the shop didn't need to stay open."

"The licensing deal depended on the shop?" Brutus had come back and was nudging her leg. He had something in his mouth, and she reached in the treat bag, hoping he hadn't slobbered all over something expensive. Brutus was happy to exchange his find for a treat, and Penelope hid what felt like a book on the seat next to her. The good news was that most of the health food books the shop sold were at a price just meant to cover the printing costs. She didn't want to distract

Skye now that she was talking. Penelope promised herself she'd come by tomorrow, when everything was open and there were more people around, and pay for it. Brutus moved away before she could grab his collar.

"You can't advertise about how 'Homespun Harold's All-Natural Emporium was founded and remains in the same location still committed to your health' if the shop closes. It's written into the contract. If I hadn't stepped in and found a way to turn a profit, my father would have had to use the licensing money just to pay the rent."

Penelope thought over what Skye had said. "I still don't see where you made your mistake."

"That makes me feel better." Skye inhaled and let the breath out slowly. "People with depression and dementia don't make big changes. They can't. So I assumed everything would just keep on the same path until the end." She mimed a train moving smoothly into the distance, and then waited.

It didn't take Penelope long to figure out what she meant. "He was going to change his will."

"How did you get there so fast?" Skye dropped her hands to the table, exasperated. "Was it really so obvious?"

"He had a book on estate planning next to his chair."

"Did he? I missed that." Skye shrugged. "But yes, suddenly he was going to change his will and leave it all to some 'save the wetlands' group. I suppose that was his revenge for the SUV and latte crowd."

"But—" Penelope stopped herself. They'd kept away from the actual murder up to this point, and she wasn't sure she should change that.

"Go ahead." Skye waved her hand again. "It's all purely hypothetical, remember?"

Brutus was back with a second book. Penelope surreptitiously traded it for another treat. The corners were worn and the pages felt wavy from water damage. She hoped he'd found a stack of books that had already been damaged and were going to be destroyed. Otherwise this talk could get expensive. "You said he was 'suddenly' changing his will."

"Oh, yes. The first I knew of it was when he said he was calling a family meeting in two days. When I said I had other things to do that day, he said I might want to know about the changes he'd made to his will."

That would have been the day before Harold's death. "But… botulism doesn't just grow in a day."

"Ah, I see. You're suggesting there was an element of planning, and that doesn't go along with my surprise he was going to change his will."

"Yes."

"Hm. You're right. Let me say that the changing of the will took me by surprise, but this wasn't the first time it had occurred to me that his death would solve a lot of my problems. Before I figured out how to lure all the people he hated into the shop, I thought I might have to go a more direct route. But then, of course, I was glad I hadn't." She glanced over at the shop windows again. "It's really too bad he didn't give me a little more warning this time. Maybe something different could have been arranged."

Penelope wondered how many times Harold had been close to death without knowing it. "It seems like such an imprecise way to get rid of someone." Brutus was back, and she took another book out of his mouth and added it to the growing pile by her leg. Skye was looking at her, so she hurried to say something to cover the movement. "I've done some canning, and I've taken classes, and the emphasis was on what *not* to do, and how important it was to properly store the jars and discard anything that went bad. But I wouldn't know how much someone would have to eat to make sure I killed them."

"You really are quite clever, aren't you? You see the difficulties." Skye was silent. Then she seemed to realize Penelope was still waiting. "Oh, you want me to... Surely you can figure that part out."

"I'm guessing it's somewhere on the internet along with how to make bombs out of vaseline and other household items." Her mind flashed back to the contents of Harold's bookshelf. "*The Anarchist's Cookbook* doesn't have a section on poisoning your enemies, does it?"

Skye laughed. "No. Have you ever read any of it? It's a sad little pamphlet with things nobody would be bothered about these days, but my father was so proud that he had it. As if it gave him some sort of credibility." She rolled her eyes. "No. One of the things you learn when you work with botanicals is that concentrations can vary wildly. I don't think the internet would be all that helpful, and it's not the sort of thing you would want showing up in your browser history, is it?"

"I suppose not."

"So... again, purely hypothetically, you could try a belt and braces approach..." She paused and gave a hint of a smile. "Or, I suppose, you could run some clinical trials." She laughed at the look on Penelope's face. "Oh, relax. I haven't left a trail of bodies for someone to find. No matter how helpful it would be to perfect the recipe before you need it, there's no point in taking that big of a risk."

The total lack of remorse made Penelope's skin prickle. Skye hadn't wanted to risk being caught before she killed her father. That was the only reason she'd held herself back. *Esther knew there was something not quite right with you*, Penelope wanted to say. But that would just make Esther another target to be knocked aside. "Even adding pain pills might not have been enough."

"Exactly!" They might have been discussing ways to swirl multiple colors together to produce a nice bar of soap. "You might have to go back and put a pillow over his face."

Could they test for something like that? For all the wrongness of the conversation, Skye hadn't told her anything that could be used to prove she had murdered her father. Brutus was back with another book. She swapped it for a treat, and stacked it with the rest, no longer worried about how much his foraging was going to cost her.

"I wondered why you... *someone* would have risked going back that night. Someone might have seen you... *them*. Or there might have been a security camera that the person didn't notice." She glanced up at the camera in the eaves.

"It's amazing how many cameras there are when you really start looking for them."

"Going back to make sure he was dead explains it. At first I thought it was just because of the alcohol, but it was so easy for the pathologist to check if he'd been drinking, that couldn't have been the only reason. Everything else felt carefully planned, but splashing alcohol around seemed like an afterthought."

"Maybe." Skye shrugged. "And yet, you know, I suspect it almost worked. Old man with a history of alcoholism dies because of sloppy canning, alcohol, and pills." She shook her head. "All those crime shows make it seem like every death is investigated, but if they did that in real life, they'd have blown through their yearly budget by the second week in January."

Penelope had once tried to watch a modern detective show with Jake in the room, but only once. The procedural errors had pained him, and then he'd given her a ballpark figure for all the tests the fictional pathologist had run. It had been larger than the city's yearly budget for school maintenance. She pushed on. "The other reason to go back would be to remove something."

Skye hummed. "Perhaps a new will."

"Like a will," Penelope agreed. "Or diaries that could be used to make someone else look guilty. But even that might not be worth the risk, especially if the person would be the one to find him later. He didn't have a large social circle. The chance of someone noticing he was missing that morning was almost zero."

Skye put her elbows on the table and leaned forward. "Since we're talking about this, how *did* you find him? And don't just say you were delivering the mail, because there's no way you could have noticed him without going behind the bushes."

"I was hiding from someone. I thought she wanted to yell at me and I was hoping to avoid a scene." If she'd known Lorna just wanted to talk about her reelection campaign, Penelope never would have found Harold, and maybe things would have gone very differently. "Then Crunch barked at me and I saw your father lying there."

Skye stared at her. "Really?" She huffed a laugh. "I thought maybe you and my father had been having an affair or something."

Penelope recoiled. "Ew. Me and Harold? Absolutely not. Ugh." She stopped, finally recognizing how rude her response had been. "I mean, I'm sure some people found him attractive..." She trailed off. She probably didn't have to justify her response to the person who had murdered him, even if her reaction had been rude.

"I wondered what else he'd been hiding from me. This makes much more sense." She leaned back. "Has anyone ever told you how inconvenient you are?"

"I'm sure there are plenty of people who think that, but most of them don't tell me."

That brought a smile to Skye's face. "Now you're making me wish we really had met under different circumstances."

"Except you probably wouldn't have noticed me," Penelope reminded her.

"True. But maybe I would have. You keep doing unexpected things. I thought you were going to be here much later tonight."

Penelope frowned. "Why?"

"It never occurred to me you would just break in while people were still around. You see? Unexpected."

"I didn't break in. The gate was open and Brutus went in while I was talking to someone." Lorna was unwittingly responsible, once again. If Penelope hadn't stopped to talk to her, she would be home already. Had it been long enough for Jake to get back? For the first time she realized how much the area had quieted while they had been talking.

"Yes, but you were *planning* to break in." When Penelope just stared at her, Skye motioned to the corner of the patio. "I heard you this morning. You said you could climb it."

"What?" Penelope thought back to the conversation she'd been having with Jake that morning. "I wasn't planning to break in. We were trying to come up with ways you could have left without ending up on the security camera. It covers the gate, but I thought you could have easily climbed the fence in that corner."

Skye gaped at her for a second, and then started laughing. "*That's* what you were doing there? I thought you were planning to break in to look for evidence." Still laughing, she looked over her shoulder at the fence corner. "Yes, I guess I probably could have climbed over that. I didn't even think about that."

"So how did you leave?" When Skye hesitated, Penelope rolled her eyes. "Purely hypothetically."

"When this building was built, the stores were bigger. They walled off the openings in the customer area when it was divided, but there's a connecting door in the stockroom and I have the key. I could go into the deli and then out through their patio."

"And just trust that nobody would check their cameras? That seems like a huge risk."

"Not really. Their cameras haven't worked for a year and a half. With the shops that have been here forever, we all know each other's phone numbers and alarm codes."

So simple. She'd just gone through a door into the next business, then straight out the back. No fence climbing had been necessary. Brutus nudged her again, and she swapped yet another damaged book for a treat. Surely he must have collected them all by now. Unless... guilt struck her. Had Skye or Harold been running a little free library? Brutus's destruction of already damaged stock was one thing, but if he'd managed to decimate an entire collection of books that people were still reading... She looked around, trying to make out the shapes on the patio in the dim light. She hadn't noticed any "take one, leave one" signs when she'd been at the soap class, but she hadn't been looking for one either.

A flicker of light in the window caught her eye. "Is that?" Penelope was on her feet and running toward the door before she finished the thought. Something on the counter was burning, but the flames were still small enough that they should be able to put them out with the fire extinguisher.

When she opened the door, a layer of thick smoke hung down from the ceiling, ending just above her head. "Where's the extinguisher?"

"On the wall behind the register."

As soon as Skye said it, Penelope remembered seeing it there. She took a deep breath and ducked down. She'd make one quick attempt to put out the fire, and if that didn't work, she'd get back out and let the firefighters handle it. Behind her, she heard the door swing shut.

She ran toward the register, eyes burning from the fumes.

The fire extinguisher wasn't there. For a long moment, she stared at the wall. The sign was there, but the red arrows pointed to a blank spot.

On the main stock table, a mound of fabric burned right next to the display of candles. The extinguisher would put that out easily, but it wasn't where it was supposed to be. Penelope wasted another few seconds looking around on the ground, then gave up. She would need to take a breath soon, and she didn't want to breathe whatever that fire was producing. She ran toward the back of the store and threw herself against the back door, ready to gulp in the fresh outside air.

The door opened a couple of inches and then slammed in her face. Penelope pushed again and it didn't budge.

At that point Penelope realized what an idiot she'd been.

All those glances toward the shop hadn't been Skye worrying she might miss a late night customer. The grill had already been pulled down over the front door and windows. Skye had been waiting for the fire she'd set to get big enough to notice. Skye hadn't been telling her things because she'd wanted to confess; she'd been feeding her just enough information to make sure Penelope didn't leave.

Penelope threw her weight against the door again. She could feel it move, so Skye hadn't wedged a piece of wood against it and left. She was probably just holding it closed by pushing against it. When Penelope succumbed to the smoke, Skye would be able to walk away, and it would just look like Penelope had collapsed by the door, unable to get any farther.

Screw that. Penelope planned to be inconvenient and unexpected for a few more decades.

She reached for her pocket, but her phone was on the table outside where she'd put it when she sat down. Lungs burning, Penelope crouched down and took a cautious breath. The air made her want to cough, but at least it was still somewhat breathable.

The front of the shop was blocked by the grill. The sides... There was an opening in the stockroom to get into the deli. Penelope crawled down the hall and pulled on the handle of the room marked *Employees Only*. The latch opened and she scrambled inside the dark room and closed the door behind her.

The air in here was better, though she could still smell smoke over the scents of molasses, musty cardboard, and patchouli. Penelope stood up and felt along the wall until she found the light switch. The fluorescents flickered and hummed to life.

The room wasn't much larger than the walk-in closets of some of her clients' homes, and the boxes stacked neatly on wire racks made it feel even smaller. Another door wasn't immediately visible, and for a moment she wondered if Skye had just made it up to keep her there. Then she realized there was a door-sized gap in the wire racks, where boxes had been stacked directly on the floor.

Penelope shifted six large boxes of silicone molds — Skye must have been making an even larger profit than Penelope had thought if the shop was going through them that quickly — and yes, there was a door. She would go through the door and out the back of the deli, and then she would flag down someone for help before she went back to get her dog and deal with Skye.

The handle didn't move.

Of course it was locked. Penelope crouched back down, trying to breathe through the panic that threatened to overwhelm her.

She had choices. She could stay in the stockroom where the air was not too bad, and hope that the fire went out on its own or that the fire department came and put it out before she suffocated. That was plan A.

She could go back out and try to keep pushing on the back door. That probably wouldn't work, but it was still an option.

What else? The front was blocked, the sides were blocked, the back door was blocked — she hit her forehead with her palm. There was a giant window overlooking the back patio. If she broke that, Skye wouldn't be able to stop her from getting out.

Penelope crouched near the door, planning her route so she didn't waste any time once she went out into the smoke-filled room. She would go left, grab the bar stool behind the register, then run down the hall and use it to bash open the window. Then she could stand on the stool and jump out. She opened the door.

During the short time she'd been in the storeroom, the smoke had dropped another foot. Penelope moved forward in a crouch, her eyes streaming. She grabbed the stool, headed to the back, and swung it against the window in a form that would have made her high school softball coach proud.

The stool bounced back and hit her in the forehead.

Penelope stumbled back, tripped, and fell on the ground. Fiberglass. She'd never felt so personally betrayed by an inanimate object before. She took another choking breath and crawled to the door. Maybe Skye had assumed she had collapsed already.

She pushed at the door, but it only gave slightly. She pushed again, and managed to knock it open just a crack, wedging her toes in the space between the door and jam. That left just a tiny sliver of open space. She leaned forward and sucked in a breath of fresh air. If she had carried a crow-bar, she'd be able to pry open the door. Grabbing her phone before running into a burning building was probably a better option. Or even just not running into a burning building.

"You'll never get away with this," Penelope rasped, stopping to cough and suck in another breath halfway through.

Skye laughed softly. She didn't even sound like she was expending any effort to hold the door closed. "Yes, I will. They'll assume you were nosy and then just as incompetent at putting out a fire as you are at everything else."

Penelope drew back her head and stared through the door to the point where Skye's face would be. "What?" Surely the woman wasn't insulting her as she tried to kill her.

"I remember you, you know. You were one of the parent helpers in first grade. You were *awful.*"

Penelope remembered those days. At the time, she'd been one of the few stay-at-home mothers, and she'd been guilted into volunteering to help, not just in her son's class, but in others as well. Usually that meant trying to assist small children fumbling their way through complicated art projects. She'd spent a lot of time trying to detach construction paper she'd inadvertently glued to her fingers.

Skye was still talking. "You made me mess up on the place mat, and then you tried to cover up the mistakes with a bunch of stickers."

Penelope pulled in another breath of fresh air. "Really? You're still holding a grudge from first grade?" She didn't remember Skye in those classes, but she *had* gone through a lot of stickers trying to convince perfectionist children that their lives weren't over just because they hadn't followed the instructions perfectly.

"Are you trying to say you've gotten better? I saw the soap you made last week." Skye laughed again. "Nobody will be surprised that you accidentally started a fire after you broke into the building. People like you are the reason I stopped having students mix their own lye."

Penelope was fairly certain that if she lived through this, she'd think up an excellent retort in about a week or two. The French had a saying for that. Something about the reply that you thought up when you were in the stairwell later.

A snuffling at the crack in the door interrupted her thought. Brutus had come over to see what was going on. "Hey, buddy." The snuffling intensified.

If they'd trained Brutus as an attack dog... Penelope's imagination couldn't make that leap. Brutus could scare people with his bark, and he was big enough to injure people while playing, but turning him into an attack dog would be beyond anyone's training abilities. He was far more dangerous to the people he loved when he was excited...

Penelope smiled.

She tried to pitch her voice higher. "Want some cheese? Huh, Brutus? Want some cheese?" She drew out the last word as much as she could. The snuffling at the door got louder, and she imagined his tail wagging.

Skye's voice was somewhere between irritated and confused. "What are you doing?"

Penelope ignored her. "Go for a walk? Have some cheese?" As with most dogs, there were certain words that Brutus knew and got excited by. Penelope normally tried not to get him too wound up in the house because all that excitement made him a big wrecking ball. He'd taken out one of the legs of the admittedly-cheap dining room table one evening when he heard Jake walking up the path.

Brutus's nose disappeared and he barked.

"Making your stupid dog bark isn't going to save you."

"Cheese? Go for a walk?" The trick was going to be getting him excited enough that he forgot most of his training. That probably wouldn't be too hard. "Do some zoomies?" Her voice was raspy from the smoke, but Brutus barked again. She heard his front claws scratch along the wall next to the door, and the jingle of his tags as he spun around.

She was only going to have one try to get this to work. Brutus tended to forget how big he was, but he learned quickly who wasn't willing to play with him. "Get some cuddles, Brutus! Cuddles!" That was the word they used when they were ready to wrestle with him.

Brutus barked again, there was a crash against the door, and then Penelope heard Skye yell. The pressure holding the door disappeared. Penelope widened the gap, ran out into the sweet air, and tripped over the dog and human rolling around on the ground in front of her.

In the distance she could hear the glorious sound of a fire engine siren.

CHAPTER 25

"She tried to kill me," Penelope repeated to Jake as they sat on the curb and let Kayden, the same firefighter she'd talked to in front of Harold's house, tape a bandage on her forehead. Her husband had just made it to the front of the shop when the fire engine rolled up, and there had been a few confusing moments when he'd been trying to force his way into the front of the building before anyone had come around the back and found Penelope, Skye, and Brutus rolling around on the ground.

Jake still didn't look quite right. Kayden had given Penelope an oxygen mask to hold over her face, and she was wondering if she ought to pass it to Jake instead. "And she made fun of my soap."

Jake turned his head to look at her. It was the first time he'd seemed to take in what she was saying. She could almost see him come back to himself. "Your orange rat-turd soap?"

"Those are lavender buds. And she called your dog stupid."

She saw him make the effort to smile. "To be fair…"

Luckily, the first firefighter to make it into the patio had been a dog lover, and he had taken Brutus's excited leap on him in the spirit it was intended. He had even stayed on his feet — though it had been a near thing — and held on long enough for Penelope to get a leash on the dog. Brutus was currently lying half on, half off the sidewalk, leaning against Jake's other side, and snoring.

The fire itself had only taken a minute to put out — fire extinguishers worked wonders when they weren't missing — but it was going to take days to get rid of the smoke damage.

The instant Skye no longer had to fend off an excited mastiff, she had thrown herself onto the shoulder of the nearest firefighter and burst into tears, babbling about a crazy stalker who had tried to burn down her shop and sicced a huge dog on her. Penelope had to give her points for the improvisation; at first glance, Skye's story held together pretty well, though it was a little light on some key details. The police officers on the graveyard shift had arrived quickly, recognized Jake and Penelope, heard the brief versions of the conflicting stories, and had decided the whole thing was a hot potato that needed to be passed along to someone else as soon as possible. Calls were made, and now they were waiting.

Penelope used the back of the hand holding the mask to tap Jake's hand. He loosened his grip. "Sorry."

"She didn't have to climb over the fence that night. There's a door connecting the storeroom to the deli, and she has the key." Well, probably *had* the key at this point. Skye had probably dumped it by now unless it was common knowledge that she had once had possession of it.

"She *told* you that?"

"With a lot of 'hypothetically, I could have done this' sprinkled in. Probably nothing that would be proof if I'd been recording our conversation." Penelope took a few breaths from the oxygen mask. "The deli's security cameras haven't worked for over a year." A fresh wave of indignation hit her. "She called me incompetent."

Jake frowned and drew his head back so he could look at her. "You?"

"Yes! Apparently she's holding a grudge from first grade when I was a parent helper." She paused as she thought about it. "She may have a point about that. The whole situation was pretty awful. Some of the teachers would pick art projects that were meant for older kids, and I spent most of the time trying to make sure nobody cut someone else's hair off, and then using stickers to hold everything together." She shrugged. "Most of the kids liked the stickers more than the art project, so I thought it had all worked out."

Kayden, still checking her head for more damage, suddenly snorted. "Wait, I remember that! You had those sheets of stickers. My mom still laughs about the flower basket made from craft paper that had all the firefighter, cowboy, and construction worker stickers. She called it the Chippendales basket." He closed up the case of first aid supplies. "I know you said you don't want to go to the hospital now, but if your breathing gets worse or anything new shows up, don't wait. Lots of fluids for the next few days." He picked up his case and looked at Jake. "Take good care of her."

"As if I'm not a grown adult —" Penelope's protests were cut off when Jake raised her hand and kissed it.

"I love you."

"I love you, too, but I still don't need anyone to tell you to take care of me, like I'm a car or …."

"Chattel?"

"Chattel! There's an old-fashioned word. I wonder if that has the same roots as cattle." She stopped and eyed him suspiciously. "You did that on purpose."

Brutus jumped to his feet as a car drove up, and Jake tightened his hold on the leash.

Penelope sighed. "I've probably ruined all his training tonight, so don't be surprised if he starts jumping on people again."

Chief Purcell climbed out of the car, looking like a man who had just been rousted from his bed. His hair stuck out on one side, and his clothes had the rumpled look of fabric that had been thrown on the floor after being taken off at the end of a long day. He drew himself up as he waited for the patrol officers to hurry forward.

Penelope could tell the exact moment when he saw her with Jake and Brutus. She watched him stiffen and take half a step back. "I don't think they told him why he was getting called to the scene."

Jake hummed agreement. "I don't miss being woken up in the middle of the night."

"I don't miss that either."

"Though I have to admit, being the reason that the chief has to be woken up in the middle of the night is not actually a whole lot better."

Penelope patted his hand. "You probably just need to get used to it."

They waited, watching Chief Purcell get briefed by his officers. He rubbed his face a lot.

Jake sighed. "He's going to tell everyone to go home for the night and come back in the morning to make a statement."

"But she tried to kill me!"

"Take the win. I had even odds on him locking you both up for the night."

Penelope subsided. Skye probably wouldn't try again overnight, and Penelope really did want a shower and clean clothes.

The patrol officers were splitting up, one to come over to them, one to talk to Skye, who was across the street wiping away delicate tears. Chief Purcell raised his voice to call after the officer coming towards Penelope. "Without that damned dog!" He got back in his car and drove off.

Penelope accepted Jake's help in standing. "He's definitely on the list of people getting orange rat-turd soap for Christmas."

"He should be so lucky."

The patrol officer relayed the order to come to the station in the morning, though Penelope suspected his wording was a lot more polite than the original version Chief Purcell had given him. "Without Brutus," he added, apologetically. "I think he might still be a little mad about the shoes."

Penelope pictured Brutus vomiting on the chief's shoes and immediately felt better. "Can I get my phone? I left it on the table in the patio."

"So you could run into a burning building." Jake's hand tightened on hers, but she didn't think it was voluntary.

"Lesson learned. Next time I'll definitely take my phone with me." She smiled as he sighed, and then they all walked around to the alley.

Aside from a metal bin of extinguished material removed from within the building, everything on the patio looked the same. But with all the lights and people, it didn't seem like such an intimate space. The firefighters would remain for a while to make sure nothing flared up, unless they were called elsewhere, though nobody seemed too worried.

Penelope's phone still lay on the table where she'd abandoned it. She pocketed it, then nearly tripped over Brutus who was sitting with intention next to the bench. Right, the books. "You already got your reward for these ones. No double dipping." She gave him another treat anyway. Without Brutus she would have been stuck in the stockroom hoping the firefighters got there before she ran out of oxygen.

She looked up at Jake. "Legal and moral question for you: If your dog damages something that may have already been damaged, are you obligated to pay the cost of replacement, even if the owner tried to kill you?" She trailed off as she got a look at the stack of books for the first time.

These weren't water-damaged books extolling the virtues of a natural diet. These were handwritten notebooks, in a spidery scrawl that looked nothing like Skye's neat printing. Each one had a year scribbled on the spine.

Penelope opened the notebook on the top of the pile, with a date from over a decade ago. The entries were a mess of scribbled notes, with dried stains making the pages cling together. She squinted, then moved the book closer to her face. It wasn't that she needed reading glasses. Handwriting was always hard to read. *Too much pepper*, said one scribble. She flipped a few more pages. *Could add more cilantro. Shelf fell. 17 jars broken. Replaced wood screws with Molly bolts.* On another page there were notes about tax forms.

Jake leaned closer to her shoulder. "What is that?"

Penelope closed the notebook and searched the rest of the pile until she found the entry for the current year. It fell open to a page halfway through when she lifted the cover, and she saw a table of dates and three columns of numbers. She saw the pattern almost immediately. The first column was always larger than the second, and the third was the difference between the two. If this showed what she thought it did, Skye had been skimming a hefty amount from the business. And Harold had known about it.

Penelope dug her phone out, took a picture of the numbers and then the last few pages with writing on them. She returned the notebook to the stack.

"I think Brian is going to want these."

CHAPTER 26

*B*y the time Brian noticed the messages on his phone and drove back from the bocce court, Penelope was ready to go home and head for bed. No matter how important all the activity at the shop was, she still needed to get up early and watch Spot so CJ could hold the morning services without the anxious wails of the Dalmatian drowning out his words.

Jake and Brian were huddled together, talking about the legalities of taking the notebooks into evidence. They were in plain sight, and discovered during the investigation of a crime, but they were only in plain sight because Brutus had dragged them to the table while Penelope and Skye had been talking. Neither man wanted the notebooks and anything Brian learned from them to be thrown out at trial.

Penelope finally pulled Jake away. "Let the people still getting paid for the job figure it out. Good night, Brian. Sorry to drag you away from the bocce game." The police could deal with making a case against Skye. Penelope was just relieved that Edward would be off the hook.

"I was losing anyhow. See you tomorrow."

Naturally, after showering off all the smoke she was more hungry than sleepy, so she headed back downstairs to the kitchen. Brutus trailed behind her, ever hopeful that she might drop some crumbs, and if that didn't happen on its own, considering if he could trip her and get the whole thing. She made a plate of cheese and crackers, avoided the dog, and sat down in her usual place on the couch. Jake had mostly recovered from his earlier fright, but she could still feel the lingering tension in his muscles when she leaned back.

Then, because her laptop was right there, she brought up the photos she'd taken of the last pages of Harold's notebook. Brian might be constrained by legalities before he could look at it, but she had no such restrictions.

From the dates on the entries, Harold hadn't been as prolific in the last few weeks of his life. Other than monitoring the finances of the shop, most of the entries had just been the date followed by a fraction, and a word or two.

She squinted at the words, absently lifting the plate with cheese and crackers so Jake could reach it. "Can you make that out?"

Jake paused to swallow his food. "I think it says *Sativa 4*. If I had to guess, that first number is a pain scale — he was having headaches, right? And then the next bit is what he used to treat it."

Armed with that knowledge, Penelope zoomed back out and looked at the last few pages. "Lots of eights and nines out of ten. He must have been miserable. No wonder his oncologist thought he was considering treatment." She enlarged one of the longer entries. Either due to the tumor or age, Harold's handwriting had gotten significantly worse in the last months of his life.

"Have you considered reading glasses?" Jake reached for another cracker.

Penelope moved the plate away from his questing hand. "I'm not that old."

"No, of course not, but at some point your nose is going to prevent you from moving things any closer to your eyes."

"Hush and tell me what that says." She moved the cheese and crackers close enough for him to reach again.

"'The quark says...' Oh wait, that's 'The *quack* says months. He means I should say my goodbyes. It means I have months to protect my leg.' That doesn't make any sense."

"It really doesn't. I saw Harold in the same pair of shorts for twenty years and his legs had nothing on yours." She reached down to pat his thigh while she looked at the screen. It really did say 'leg'. That part was legible enough for her to read. "I'm guessing that's supposed to be *legacy*."

"That makes more sense. '... months to protect my legacy. *Something something* an addict and a thief. They deserve nothing.' That's the part that is underlined three times."

Penelope frowned. "Remind me to leave a nicer note for Seth if I'm about to die. Angry rantings just make the writer seem like an ass."

"I'm fairly certain your son already knows you love him." He scrolled to see the other entries. "The rest of it looks like more of the same. I don't see anything that says he definitely wrote a will, but there's a lot of stuff that makes it look like the dog was going to get it all if he did."

"Imagine being more worried that your kids don't get anything they don't deserve than helping them. Though I do understand making sure the dog isn't homeless." She stretched her toes under Brutus's shoulder, and he interrupted his snoring long enough to lick his nose before settling again.

"The only way our dog would become homeless is because he caused enough structural damage to the house that we couldn't live here anymore." He took the empty plate from her and stood up, pushing cushions into place so she could keep leaning back. "Do you want more crackers?"

"No. Breakfast is only a few hours away." Penelope closed the laptop and followed him into the kitchen. "Do you think there's enough evidence to charge Skye?"

"Maybe. They'll be going over her place carefully now. I'd be surprised if there wasn't something there. People think they've gotten rid of everything, but they never do." He started washing the few dishes in the sink, so Penelope picked up the dish towel.

"Do you know what I was thinking when I was stuck in that storeroom?"

Jake turned his head to look at her, ignoring the water still running in the sink. "With anyone else I'd be expecting something about all the things you regretted you didn't have a chance to say, but somehow…"

Penelope smiled and stood on her toes to kiss his cheek. "You know me well." She waited until he had turned forward and started washing again. "Besides, I was still too mad about Skye holding the back door closed to be maudlin." She took the plate he handed her and dried it. "No, I was thinking that I really should have learned how to pick locks. If I had, I could have just gone straight through to the deli and gotten away."

"*That's* your takeaway from this evening? That you should have learned lock picking?"

"You have to admit, it's more practical than learning to make soap. Do you think there are classes for it?" She watched as he started his careful routine of wiping down the sink and counters. "Do you know someone? Or…" Penelope let her voice drop. "You already know how, don't you?"

"It causes a lot less damage than breaking a window or kicking in the door when someone calls to say their mother hasn't answered the phone in three days."

"I *knew* I should have taken you with me when I went over to look through Harold's windows the other night."

"I was too busy organizing and restocking the freezer." He grinned as he finished with the sink.

Penelope opened the freezer door. Instead of the jumbled mess of poorly-labeled leftovers and foil balls that had been opened so many times that they no longer protected the freezer-burned contents, there was a neat stack of packages, each with a label describing the contents and the date. The mystery packages that Penelope was afraid to throw out in case it was something important were all gone.

That should have left a lot of free space, but the lower two shelves were now taken over by plastic bins containing stuffed dog treats. Penelope held one up and let the freezer door close.

"They were on sale."

She nodded. "Before I commend you on your purchases, this isn't the start of a decline where I can't send you to the store without you buying twelve boxes of a cereal brand we never eat just because it's on sale, is it?"

"Not yet. The efficiency of a freezer increases when it's full."

Penelope cleared her throat. "I see. So this was all about efficiency."

"Absolutely."

Penelope nodded. "Don't imagine that I'm going to forget about lock picking, but I think we might need to go upstairs to have a conversation about efficiency."

"I'll check the doors and meet you up there."

CHAPTER 27

*A*fter a morning of giving her statement at the police station and then catching up on her dog walking duties, it was late afternoon before Penelope was able to stop in at Esther's. With the client's permission, Jake had taken over the usual jog with Heidi, since Penelope's throat was still a little raw from the smoke. Esther's cats could have handled waiting another day to have their litter boxes cleaned, but Penelope knew Esther would have questions for her.

Everyone knew Skye had been arrested and charged with arson and the attempted murder of Penelope. Esther would have more information than Penelope about when Skye would be charged with Harold's murder, but Penelope knew she had a duty to fill in the details.

Esther opened the door and waved her in. "Edward and Tweetie will probably be here soon, so if you have anything to tell me that you don't want to say in front of them, now's the time." She tapped a box on the table. "I have a broken vase for him to glue back together."

Penelope leaned forward and lifted one flap. Porcelain

shards, all roughly the same size, filled the box. She took out one piece and looked at the colors. It didn't fit with anything else in Esther's house. "What did you do, go to the thrift shop, buy an old vase, and smash it with a hammer?" She'd meant it as a joke, but Esther's expression of guilt, quickly smoothed away, made her laugh. "Esther!"

"It was so ugly they practically paid me to take it away."

"And Edward talks more when he has something to do with his hands."

Esther frowned at her. "Edward is more *comfortable* when he has something to do with his hands. He was the same way as a small child. His sister tried to frame him for their father's murder. He could probably use some comfort now." She poured Penelope a glass of lemonade. "She really tried to keep you in the shop while it burned down?"

Penelope dropped the shard back in the box and sat down at the table. "I don't know if the building would have caught fire, but the smoke certainly could have killed someone."

Penelope recounted the evening to Esther, finishing with an explanation of the notebooks that Brutus had uncovered. "She'd probably hidden them well, but they must have had the scent we'd been using to train Brutus. Harold used his diaries to keep track of everything — he had notes on recipes and essential oil blends. To a dog's nose they must have a little bit of everything. Anyhow, while Skye was waiting for the fire to be big enough for me to notice and stupidly go try to put out, Brutus just kept bringing me her father's diaries."

Esther frowned as she finished. "I just don't understand why she would keep them at all. And if she did keep them, why at the shop? Why not hide them in a place less public?"

"Keeping them at the shop makes some sense, at least until she used one to implicate Edward. It was Harold's shop, after all. Who's to say he didn't leave them there himself? After she hid one under Edward's porch, it probably wasn't worth the risk to move them. They hadn't been found up to that point, so they probably weren't going to be."

"She hadn't counted on Brutus."

"Exactly." Penelope drank more lemonade. Her throat still ached from the smoke. "To be fair, I wouldn't have counted on Brutus either. I'd have assumed he was far more likely to eat the diaries than bring them to me." She thought about the evening and laughed. "Skye must have been so pleased that she was managing to keep me from leaving while waiting for the fire to be large enough to notice, and in the meantime, there was Brutus, bringing me one diary after another."

The doorbell rang, and Esther went to answer it. When she came back, Edward and Tweetie were with her. After everyone had greeted each other, Edward sat down and pulled the box of vase fragments toward him. Tweetie picked up a piece. A furrow formed between her eyebrows, and she looked around the room.

Edward selected three pieces that formed a large section of the base. "My mom called this afternoon. We're going out to brunch tomorrow."

"Is this the first time you've seen her since you were released?" Esther handed the tube of glue to Tweetie.

"No, we've had coffee a few times, but I think it was always at times when Rick was out of town." He glanced up. "Rick is her husband." Then he looked back down and held out one piece for Tweetie to glue. "I got the feeling on the phone today that she's leaving him. I hope so."

Tweetie nodded. "We're going to try to get her to spend some time at my parents' winery. They have a guest house that is empty at the moment, and that would give my mom something to focus on other than our wedding." She gave Esther a wry look. "She's been really great lately, with finding a lawyer for Edward and taking his father's dog until everything calms down, but in two days we're going to be back to a constant stream of texts about whether some flower is really purple enough to be part of the table decorations."

"We could always elope." Edward held out another piece for her to put glue on. Then he brightened. "Or get her to help with the emporium. My mom hates that place, but if Skye... Someone is going to have to keep it going, at least until it can be sold." He looked up at Penelope and Esther. "I'll help, but..."

"But you have your own complicated relationship with the place," Tweetie finished for him. "Getting my mom involved is a genius idea. And my dad could sit in a chair and tell the customers that they wouldn't need so much fiber in their diet if they just discussed things with their therapist." She exchanged a private grin with Edward, then looked up. "My dad is a character."

"Your dad is great." Edward tore off a box flap and set the assembled base on it. "The probate is probably going to drag on forever though." He pulled two more shards from the box. "There may be another will, if my dad got around to drawing it up, and if my sister didn't destroy it."

Penelope thought back to her conversation with Skye the night before. Skye hadn't actually admitted to finding another will, at least not as far as Penelope could remember. "What happens if nobody finds it?" There were notes in his diary about leaving it all to Crunch, but surely that wouldn't be used.

"Presumably they go with the last will he signed. I think that one left everything to my mom and Skye, though I'm guessing Skye's share won't go to her if she goes to prison for killing him." He shrugged. "I knew I was never going to get any part of it, but hopefully my mom will end up with enough that she doesn't have to worry about anything."

Esther was watching the vase being reassembled with a grimace, as if it had suddenly dawned on her that if Edward managed to piece it all back together, she was going to have to display it in her house. Penelope smiled at the thought. Esther deserved to have her chickens come home to roost.

That thought reminded Penelope of the earlier conversation. "Do you mind if I ask a question?"

"Go for it. You kept me from being arrested again. What do you want to know?" The vase was starting to take shape, and Edward held out another piece for Tweetie to put glue on.

"Do you have any idea why Skye kept your dad's journals? Even after she used one to incriminate you, she still didn't destroy the rest of them."

"That one I *can* answer. My dad kept everything in his journals — recipes, passwords, contact details for the guy who will come retrieve a beehive from a wall, that sort of thing. She was probably afraid of destroying some important information if she didn't go through them first, and his handwriting was hard enough to read that it was going to take a while."

"I thought it might be something like that." Penelope got to her feet. "I need to go take care of the cats."

She was scooping around the nosy tuxedo in the final litter box when Tweetie slipped into the room and closed the door behind her.

"I just wanted to say thank you, again. Not just for keeping Edward out of jail, but... I don't think he realizes — even now — what lengths his sister would go to. She's his big sister, you know?"

Penelope nodded. "She didn't seem bothered much by her first murder. I imagine a second would be even easier." Esther had pointed out the problem right after Harold's death. Skye had been good at setting up Edward to take the blame for everything. That hadn't been good for Edward, but it hadn't been good for Skye either. "I don't know if going to prison is going to be enough to deter Skye from doing it again, even if she is convicted."

"In some ways I feel sorry for her. But…."

"But not enough to want her living near you," Penelope supplied with a nod.

"Exactly."

They made their way back out to the kitchen so Penelope could wash her hands. Edward was just fitting the last shard into place. "There. Good as new."

Penelope paused in drying her hands to look at it. She could see why the thrift store had found it difficult to sell. A red, white, and blue eagle clutching a bible in its talons dove toward a rabbit on the ground. Fighter jets soared in the blue sky behind the bird.

Edward picked it up. "Shall I throw it away now?"

Esther's face was a mixture of chagrin and relief. "Yes, please. Thank you, Edward."

CHAPTER 28

When Penelope made it home, the house was empty, but the smell of lasagna made her mouth water. She heard noises in the backyard.

"Who wants some cuddles?" Jake laughed and grunted a little. He was still on his feet when Penelope looked out. Then he looked up at the sound of the door opening and Brutus seized his chance, slamming into the back of Jake's knees and wheeling and standing over him on the ground. He leaned forward and licked Jake's face.

Penelope leaned against the house. "You okay down there?"

"Just fine." Jake reached up with one arm and rolled himself and the dog across the grass a few times, flung himself to the side and jumped to his feet before Brutus could pounce on him again. "See?" He was slightly out of breath, but laughing.

Penelope regarded him. Normally by this point in the day his face looked slightly tense, as if he didn't have a headache yet, but one might strike at any minute. She realized she hadn't seen that look in the past few days.

Jake looked down at his shirt. "What's wrong? Did I roll in something?"

"No, nothing like that." She brushed some grass off his back. "I was just thinking how much retirement seems to suit you."

"Give it a few months. You may get sick of me." The oven timer went off and he ushered her inside, leaving Brutus to keep digging the ever-expanding hole in the corner of the yard. "But I was thinking about things today while I was running."

"How'd that go?"

"The thinking or the running?" He grinned and pulled on the pink frog oven mitts, a homemade gift from his aunt. "That German Shepherd, Heidi, just ran right next to me the entire time."

"It's a nice change from Brutus, isn't it?"

"My knees were happy about it." He pulled a pan of lasagna from the oven and set it on the stove. "Anyhow, I was thinking that some days you have so much work that you have to turn people away, and maybe I could help out. With the paperwork at least, even if you don't want me to do anything else."

Penelope kept her face straight with an effort. "You want to work for me?"

He paused, as if he hadn't considered it like that. "Yes?"

"Good. I've never had an intern before."

"I'm an intern?"

"The pay is terrible, but the benefits are great." She stood on her toes to kiss his cheek. "And it will still give you time to teach me how to pick locks."

He got out silverware to put on the table. "I was hoping you had forgotten about that."

"Not a chance. I need to get moving on my life of crime or I'm going to be too old to climb up to second story windows." She glanced at the backyard. "Did you feed the big guy yet?"

"Not yet."

Brutus abandoned his digging at the sound of the first kibble hitting his bowl. Moving to the side so he wouldn't barrel through her, Penelope patted his shoulder as he went by. Over at the table, Jake hummed the opening bars of *That's Amore*, the clank of a knife providing the rhythm as it cut through slightly burned lasagna in the measured beats of a waltz.

Penelope smiled. It was the end of another perfect day.

ACKNOWLEDGMENTS

One of the best parts about being an author is that you can message people for help in killing someone with botulism and they won't call the police. A huge thank you goes to Jennifer Crawford who knits, bakes, fosters kittens, *and* answered all my canning questions. Everything I got right is due to her; any screw-ups are my own fault.

I remain grateful to all of my critique partners, both in WF and YWC. They point out plot holes, find scenes that need a little tweaking, and most importantly, provide support and encouragement.

Finally, thank you to my brother, Eric, for catching the final typos. He says he enjoys it because it's his chance to point out things that I'm doing wrong. It's good to know that sibling rivalry has a purpose all these years later.

ABOUT THE AUTHOR

Tess Baytree is the pen name of speculative fiction author T. M. Baumgartner. At various times she has been a veterinarian, Unix system administrator, software developer, and after-hours book-shelver in a medical library.

Theresa currently lives in Northern California in a house with too many animals. She knits hats for garden gnomes and runs with scissors only when absolutely necessary.

Want updates about new releases? Silly dog anecdotes? Join the newsletter mailing list! Go to https://tmbaumgartner.com/subscribe/ or point your phone's camera at the QR code above.